The intimacy was undermining

Lauren stood at the door in an obvious way, and Sam turned, his mouth leashed, and walked toward her.

She stiffened as he drew level with her, her back against the wall, her head up, her mouth dry. Every nerve in her body seemed to be twanging like a taut guitar string as he paused, staring down into her eyes with a hypnotic intensity.

"One day you and I are going to have a showdown," he bit out, his brows threatening. Then he walked past, and she sagged against the wall in relief as she heard the front door slam.

CHARLOTTE LAMB is one of Harlequin's best-loved and bestselling authors. Her extraordinary career, in which she has written more than one hundred books, has helped shape the face of romance fiction around the world.

Born in the East End of London, Charlotte spent her early childhood moving from relative to relative to escape the bombings of World War II. After working as a secretary in the BBC's European department, she married a political reporter who wrote for *The Times*. Charlotte recalls that it was at his suggestion that she began to write, "because it was one job I could do without having to leave our five children." Charlotte and her family now live in a beautiful home on the Isle of Man. It is the perfect setting for an author who creates characters and stories that delight romance readers everywhere.

Books by Charlotte Lamb

HARLEQUIN PRESENTS
1467—HEART ON FIRE
1480—SHOTGUN WEDDING

BARBARY WHARF
1498—BESIEGED
1509—BATTLE FOR POSSESSION
1513—TOO CLOSE FOR COMFORT
1522—PLAYING HARD TO GET
1530—A SWEET ADDICTION
1540—SURRENDER

Charlotte Lamb

SLEEPING PARTNERS

Harlequin Books

TORONTO • NEW YORK • LONDON
AMSTERDAM • PARIS • SYDNEY • HAMBURG
STOCKHOLM • ATHENS • TOKYO • MILAN
MADRID • WARSAW • BUDAPEST • AUCKLAND

Harlequin Presents Plus first edition June 1993
ISBN 0-373-11560-1

Original hardcover edition published in 1991
by Mills & Boon Limited

SLEEPING PARTNERS

CHAPTER ONE

IT WAS Rob who first noticed the other couple sitting in a corner of the crowded wine-bar. 'Isn't that your friend Patty over there?' he asked Lauren, who was busy trying to catch the waiter's eye to remind him that they had asked for their bill. The young man was on his own tonight, and trying to do too much at once; he didn't even look their way, although normally, when she was eating here, he hovered around Lauren like a fly around a honeypot.

She rarely had trouble getting a waiter's attention; blonde, green-eyed, with a good figure, she more often attracted attention she could do without, but tonight she was in a hurry. She hadn't finished work yet; she would have to get back to the office and finish a long article about women's lingerie through the ages, in time to meet a ten o'clock deadline. The magazine went to the printer at ten-thirty, and it was already past eight.

'Patty?' she said, though, turning back towards Rob with an immediate smile. 'Where?' She and Patty were close friends; they had worked on the same magazine together until six months ago, then Patty had moved on elsewhere, but they still met, at the leisure centre they both used, in the swimming-pool or the gym, at parties, or for lunch. Theirs was a small world: London journalists mostly knew each other, by name or sight, if not in fact, and many friendships cut across professional loyalty to a paper.

'Behind the artificial palm trees to your right,' Rob said, and Lauren looked that way, and got a shock.

'I don't believe it!' she said, taken aback.

'Isn't it her?' Rob asked in surprise, and she pulled a face, nodding grimly.

'Oh, it's her!'

'I thought it was! And who's the guy with her? It isn't her husband, is it?'

'No,' said Lauren, clipping the words out, her eyes as sharp as knives as she stared at the other couple. 'It isn't.'

'I was sure it wasn't,' said Rob, looking pleased with himself. He notoriously couldn't remember faces unless he knew them very well, which could be a big handicap, especially to someone who met a lot of people every day, and was expected to remember them. 'I remember Louis Saville quite well. I've met him a few times, and I thought that wasn't him, although this guy is dark too, and around the same height. But you know what a rotten memory I have; I thought maybe I was mistaken and that was Patty's husband.'

'No, that isn't Louis,' Lauren said absently, watching Patty glowing and leaning forward to smile at the man opposite her, her brown eyes dilated with an excitement Lauren could feel right across the room. 'Patty must be out of her mind!'

'Do you get the same feeling I get?' asked Rob with amused interest. 'That she's got something going with this guy? I wonder who he is?'

'I know who he is,' Lauren said with what sounded remarkably like venom. 'It's Sam Hardy!'

'Sam Hardy?' It was Rob's turn to sound taken aback, his jaw dropping. 'The war photographer?'

'There's only one Sam Hardy,' Lauren said tightly.

Rob stared across the room at the other man. 'So,' he said slowly, 'that's Sam Hardy. I've never actually seen him before in the flesh, just his photo in the paper now and then. Dad's very proud of him, you know. He won Photographer of the Year twice in succession, and regularly scoops the other papers with pictures they completely miss. Dad says he has a nose for news; he can smell where it's happening, and gets there just at the right time. He wouldn't part with Sam Hardy for a million pounds. When he got shot up in Lebanon Dad had him flown back in the private jet with a top medical team in attendance. He couldn't have done more for one of the family, he thinks Sam Hardy's one hell of a guy.'

Lauren's expression was irritated. 'Well, Patty's crazy if she's got mixed up with him. I thought she had more sense. She knows what he's like. He's famous for what he does to women. He's only been back in England since last October. Six months! And he's already swept through London like flu. It doesn't last long, and it isn't fatal—but it leaves them weak at the knees for quite a while, so I'm told.'

Rob laughed aloud, but then gave her a curious look. 'You know, you sound very personal about him—have you had this flu, Lauren?'

Her darkened lashes briefly lowered over those slanting, misty green eyes, then lifted again, and she gave him a wry, smiling shrug. 'Oh, I felt it coming on once, but I took precautions and managed to escape the worst.'

Rob looked amused: he wasn't the jealous type; he didn't need to be! He was blond too, but his hair was a shade richer, a golden colour, and his eyes were the colour of new hazelnuts, a yellowy-green. Rob was beautiful; slim and supple, always smoothly dressed, with a very sexy body. He had never had to fear competition or lack confidence. In fact, he was almost too sure of himself, and with good reason. He had been born lucky; one of those men who seemed to have everything. Looks, charm, money had been showered on him at birth, and it was a mystery to Lauren why he had picked her out of all the far more beautiful women he could have had.

Unfortunately, it was a mystery to his father too; an unpleasant one. He was refusing even to meet her, let alone accept her as a future daughter-in-law, and she couldn't really blame him—after all, she was an ordinary working girl, with no wealthy family connections. Charles Cornwell was a Press baron, with a whole quiverful of newspapers across the country; he must have hoped, or indeed planned, for an important marriage for his only son, the heir to so much money and power.

Lauren sighed briefly. Oh, well, Rob was confident he could talk his father round. He had never failed to get his own way with Charles Cornwell yet, so maybe he was right to be complacent, but it worried her to be the cause of a rift between father and son. It was the only shadow in her blue sky at the moment. She hadn't been this happy for years, and she was scared something might happen to shatter this happiness.

'So,' Rob said lightly, 'you're the one that got away, are you?'

'By the skin of my teeth,' she agreed, smiling back. 'And the best of it is, I'm immunised—I'm safe from now on!'

Rob raised an eyebrow teasingly. 'Well, I hope so, darling!' But it was all fun; he wasn't scared of losing her to any other man. Rob had never lost anything he wanted, to anyone. He had been spoilt all his life.

'You don't get an attack of Sam Hardy twice,' Lauren said calmly. 'Well, nobody ever has! And I don't intend to be the first!' She looked across the room at the other couple. 'I can't believe Patty would be silly enough to get involved with him either.'

'Maybe they just ran into each other, and shared a table?' suggested Rob. 'Or they're on the same job, and discussing tactics?'

'Maybe,' said Lauren. 'But it doesn't look like business to me.' Patty was looking across the table as if she could eat the man sitting opposite her.

'Well, if you're right, let's hope Louis doesn't find out,' said Rob as the waiter finally materialised with their bill.

Lauren frowned, her face sober. She liked Louis
Saville, as much as she liked his wife. She was still
working with him, because Louis was marketing director with *Ultra* magazine, which was one reason why
Patty had decided to switch jobs. It wasn't always a
good idea for husband and wife to work together;
there could be problems. She had confided to Lauren
that she felt she was seeing too much of Louis during
the day; they never seemed to get away from each
other, and you could have too much even of a very
good thing, she had grimaced.

Maybe something had already gone wrong with that
marriage before Sam Hardy turned up? All the same,
it still upset Lauren to think of their marriage breaking apart, especially over someone like Sam Hardy.
She would have said that Patty and Louis Saville were
perfectly matched: Patty was delicate, pretty and sensitive; Louis was shrewd, clever, tough-minded. They
dovetailed—and yet the perfect marriage obviously
wasn't really perfect, or why had Sam Hardy ever got
anywhere with Patty?

'Shall we go, then?' asked Rob, on his feet after
paying the waiter.

Lauren started out of her absorption, nodded and
got up, collecting her bag and buttoning the elegant
jacket of her black suit with one long-fingered hand.

It was a warm spring evening, and they had walked
across the road to the wine-bar from the ground sky-
scraper building housing most of the Cornwell na-
tional magazines and newspapers. It was only two
minutes from door to door; she hadn't needed a coat.

Rob watched her, his hazel eyes caressing. 'You look very sexy,' he murmured softly.

She fluttered her lashes at him. 'Thank you. So do you.'

He grinned. 'You're also a flirt!'

'Snap!' she said, and they both laughed, because it was a game they often played and at which they were both quite good. Flirting was fun, even when you were very much in love, and serious about it.

'You come along with me, miss!' Rob said mock-sternly, put an arm around her slender waist and guided her to the door—where they walked straight into Patty and Sam Hardy.

Lauren hadn't even seen them move from their table. She stopped dead, and so did Patty, flushing to her hairline and unable to meet Lauren's eyes.

Lauren got the feeling Patty would have liked to bolt out of the door like a terrified rabbit, but Sam was holding her elbow and probably wouldn't let go. He wasn't bothered by running into someone who knew them both, which didn't surprise Lauren.

Nothing ever ruffled Sam Hardy; he prided himself on being ultra-cool, even under fire. That was how he had got shot in Lebanon—he had been somewhere dangerous, taking pictures, when any sane man would have been hiding behind a wall. Well, he was going to need that cool nerve when Patty's husband found out what had been going on behind his back!

'Well, well, look who's here!' he drawled, letting those hard grey eyes travel over Lauren in an open assessment of her body that made her stiffen with affront. 'Long time, no see. How are you?'

'I'm fine,' she bit out, without asking after his own health, and he grinned mockingly.

'The suit's a knockout.'

'Thank you,' she said through her teeth, resenting the way his eyes were lingering on Rob's arm around her waist.

Sam Hardy quickly looked up, right into Lauren's angry green eyes before she could look away or veil their expression. He said softly: 'But I must ask ... I bet every man who sees you in it is dying to know—are you wearing anything under it? It looks as if you aren't.'

In fact, it wasn't the sort of outfit you wore with a neat white blouse. It was soft silk jersey, and clung to every line of her; stylishly cut, with deep lapels in a V-neck, a tight waist with a little peplum flaring out from it, and a smooth, straight skirt. She had bought it in Paris a month ago—it had cost the earth, but it looked so good on her that for once she didn't care.

It looked as if it were her outer skin. All she had on under it was lingerie, very delicate, silky, lacy black lingerie, which she had also bought in Paris, and it really burned Lauren up to know that Sam Hardy was speculating on what she looked like in it. She hated the way he undressed her with those insolent eyes, but she wasn't going to have a row with him over it in a bar used by so many people from their company.

When you confronted Sam Hardy it was wise to do it on territory of your own choosing, in your own good time, so all she did now was ignore his question and turn her eyes to Patty, who was watching her, brown eyes over-bright and defiant.

'Hello, Patty,' Lauren said flatly.

'Hi,' Patty muttered, looking away. Her eyes just happened to fall on Rob, who grinned at her.

'Hi—remember me?'

Patty, if it was possible, looked even more panic-stricken. 'I . . . y—yes, of course. Rob Cornwell, isn't it? We met at Lauren's party a couple of months ago.'

'That's right,' he encouraged. 'I was the guy pouring the drinks and washing up glasses afterwards.'

'And doing the odd bit of drinking in between,' Lauren said, and he made a face at her.

'Don't nag, woman! What are parties for?' He turned his grin towards Sam Hardy, and held out the hand which wasn't holding Lauren's waist. 'Women are the policemen of the sexes, aren't they? Always laying down the law and trying to put us behind bars.' His comradely grin did not meet with much response from Sam, who considered him drily without saying anything, and Rob said uncertainly, 'I don't think we've met before, have we? I'm Rob Cornwell— I've heard a lot about you, of course. My father thinks you're the world's greatest photographer.'

'Then he might raise my salary,' Sam Hardy said, and Rob laughed shortly, taken aback by that, and quickly changed the subject in a rather obvious way.

'How are you settling down in London now you're here most of the time? I expect you miss travelling around, don't you?'

'Yes,' said Sam curtly.

'My father said something about your injury keeping you here for the moment? You have to go in to hospital for weekly treatment?'

Sam nodded, his mouth a straight line. He hated talking about his personal life, Lauren remembered—how long would it take Rob to get the message? The trouble was, Rob was spoilt by too many years of being his father's son. Even genuine interest sounded in his light voice like patronage, and a man like Sam Hardy resented being patronised.

Studying him from under her lowered lashes, she realised why Rob was talking about his illness. At close quarters, she could see the changes his injury had brought about in him. He was thinner, paler, a darkness shadowing his eyes. She glimpsed tension in the hard mouth, the line of the jaw, the taut stretch of skin across the cheekbones. Sam did not look at all well.

Frowning, she shot Patty a sideways look. 'Walk across the road with me, will you, Patty? I want a private word.'

Patty looked uneasy, but fell into step beside her as she began to cross the road. The two men strolled behind, just far enough for Lauren to have the chance of asking in a low voice, 'Are you crazy, Patty? What on earth is going on with you and Sam Hardy?'

'We were both having dinner,' Patty said defensively. 'Why shouldn't we eat it together? We do work for the same outfit, remember?'

'I remember,' said Lauren. 'But I'm not blind—I saw the way you were looking at him back there.'

Patty was crimson and stuttering. 'I... I wasn't...'

'Don't try to kid me!' snapped Lauren. 'And don't kid yourself either. No woman dates a guy like Sam Hardy and manages to keep it platonic—he doesn't play that sort of game. Are you really ready to throw away a good marriage for a man like him?'

Patty stopped in her tracks and burst out angrily, 'Good marriage? To a man who's never home and never sees me? Louis lives for his work, I don't matter a damn to him.' She bit down on her lower lip, glaring. 'And anyway, what business is it of yours what I do? Don't you lecture me, Lauren Bell!'

The men had caught up with them and were standing there, listening to the tail-end of Patty's outburst. Rob raised his brows at Lauren, grimacing, but Sam Hardy gave her a lazy, mocking smile.

'Giving Patty good advice, Lauren?'

'That's right,' she said in a breathless, impeded voice. 'And I hope she takes it!'

He slid an arm around Patty, holding her shoulders. 'Will you, Patty?'

She leaned on him, her brown eyes glowing like amber lamps. 'I doubt it; I don't need Lauren telling me what to do! I can do my own thinking.'

He turned his gaze on Lauren again, one brow lifted in dry comment. 'Too bad. It looks as if you wasted your time, doesn't it?'

A taxi was cruising towards them, its For Hire sign lit. Sam raised a hand and the taxi swooped sideways to pull up beside the kerb.

Opening the rear door, Sam helped Patty clamber into the back of the cab. She didn't even look back at Lauren and Rob, let alone say goodnight to them, just sat down, crossing her long, silk-clad legs, her face averted, in stony profile.

Sam gave them a glance, nodded casually to them both, but said to Lauren as he walked past her, 'Going to take your own advice, are you?' before getting into the taxi beside Patty.

Lauren's teeth met and her hands curled in helpless frustration. He was implying that she would now go back with Rob and sleep with him, and she would love to shout a furious denial, but she couldn't. Oh, it wasn't true—she was going back to work, not home to bed with Rob—but that wasn't the point. She wasn't getting bogged down in an argument with Sam Hardy on the subject. It was none of his business—and that was something else he had been implying. He meant that what he and Patty did was none of hers!

But their situation was very different. She and Rob were going to be married. Patty was already married—to another man. And Sam Hardy was going the right way about destroying her marriage, without being serious about Patty either, if Lauren knew him. He had never been serious about anyone in his life—except himself.

The taxi drove away while she was still seething, but she had heard the address Sam gave the driver, and recognised it. They were going to Patty's flat in Knightsbridge, which merely confirmed what Lauren had suspected, a confirmation she could have done without.

'Where is her husband, anyway?' asked Rob, staring after the red tail-lights of the taxi.

'In Glasgow,' Lauren answered. 'Working. He isn't due back for two days.' Did he suspect anything yet? She was almost certain Louis did not know; Patty would have told her if he did. No, Louis had yet to find out—how long would it be before one of his 'friends' told him? Or some girl who didn't like Patty, or did, perhaps, rather like Louis, and feel he ought to know his wife was cheating? Sooner or later someone would tell him.

Rob whistled. 'Poor old Louis!' His tone was faintly contemptuous rather then sympathetic. He thought Patty's husband must be weak, a fool, if he let her run around with other men, especially men like Sam Hardy.

He eyed Lauren, grimacing. 'I see what you meant about Hardy, though. He is a tough guy, isn't he? He was telling me he still had shrapnel in his back; the doctors are leaving it there to work its own way out, and he says it hurts like hell at night when he's lying down.'

'Good!' said Lauren, meaning it, and Rob laughed, looking surprised.

'You really hate him, don't you?'

'I don't like him,' she agreed.

Rob wasn't stupid; he stared thoughtfully, his brows up. 'Darling, you aren't still carrying a torch, are you?'

She was taken aback this time, her eyes widening in shock and anger. 'For Sam Hardy? I'm not that crazy!' She put her arms around his neck and smiled up at him, her body leaning against his. 'The only torch I'm carrying is for you, Rob.'

He put his arms round her too, his eyes smiling. 'I'm glad about that, darling; I wouldn't want to have to find Sam Hardy and strangle him.'

'The only way to kill a vampire is drive a stake through his heart,' Lauren said, then pulled Rob's head down towards her. 'Can we stop talking about him? We have better things to do than that.'

Rob agreed. He didn't waste any more words; their mouths met with a passion that put everything else out of their minds, and when they did move apart they were both breathing thickly and looking faintly dazed.

'Wow!' Rob muttered unsteadily. 'That torch of yours certainly starts a blaze!' His eyes moved over her face, eagerness in that look. 'Do you have to go back to work? Can't whatever you have to do wait until tomorrow? We could go back to your flat and carry on from here.'

'Don't tempt me!' Lauren wanted to do just that; she wanted it badly, her green eyes leaping with feeling, but she shook her head wryly and let her arms fall. 'Darling, I'd love it, but I need my job, and if I don't get my work finished in time for that deadline I'll find myself unemployed tomorrow. You know Annie Jones—she's a very tough editor and she doesn't forgive mistakes.'

'You're marrying the boss's son, remember!' Rob said with a touch of arrogance that made her frown. He was usually so careful not to pull rank. She had been impressed by his tact and discretion with other members of staff from the first day they met, at a Christmas party given by Annie Jones herself. Rob had been there representing his father; a gesture of congratulation to Annie, who had been delighted. Everyone had known, of course, who he was, and had been wary of him, but Rob had gone out of his way to put them at their ease, chatting lightly and cheerfully, behaving as if he were just another employee. He wasn't, and everyone knew it, but Rob had made himself popular with most people by trying, and Lauren was upset to hear him talking in this way now.

'Tell her you were with me, and she won't dare say another word,' he said impatiently, and no doubt he was right. Annie Jones would be put in an impossible situation if Lauren followed Rob's advice. Lauren frowned, watching his handsome face, the restless hazel eyes, the irritable curve of the mouth.

Gently, she said, 'I can't do that, darling. It wouldn't be fair. She has her job to do, and I'm not asking for special favours just because I'm dating the boss's son.' She watched the clouding over of his face and sighed. 'Darling, what if she went to your father about it? Do you think he'd back me up? You know I'm not exactly flavour of the month with him! He'd be more likely to jump at the chance to get rid of me.'

'He'd have me to deal with if he did!' Rob flared, but his eyes told her that she had touched a nerve. He knew his father would back the editor, not her, and quite right too, Lauren thought honestly. After all, why should she be able to demand special favours because she was going to marry one of the Cornwell family? It wouldn't make her popular with anyone in the organisation if it got out. People would steer clear of her in future; they would feel they couldn't trust her or rely on her.

Of course, Charles Cornwell would have other reasons for backing Annie Jones; he would be delighted to be given such an excellent excuse for sacking her.

'We don't want a war with your father, do we, Rob?' she asked him in a pleading voice, and Rob's mouth turned down at the edges in boyish dissatisfaction.

He looked into her coaxing face, then sighed and shrugged reluctantly. 'OK, darling, have it your way— but you'd better not be working late tomorrow night! I have plans for you and me tomorrow, and don't forget it!'

'I won't!' Her green eyes promised pleasure, and Rob's body relaxed; he smiled down at her.

'I can't wait!'

They separated a moment later; Rob to collect his car from the underground car park and Lauren to walk into the marble-floored lobby of the building where they both worked. Even at this hour of the evening the place was busy with people; the night staff of the various newspapers had all begun work and some of the day staff still hadn't left. Lauren took the lift up to her own floor and a moment later was at her desk, picking up work where she had left off. She called her article back on to the screen of her word-processor, read it through and was soon busy finishing it.

She had been working on *Ultra* for a couple of years now, and was beginning to know the seasonal routine by heart. They worked several months ahead, to fit in with publishing schedules, so that in October they were already working on the Christmas issue, and now, in April, they were dealing with the June magazine, which, for this as for every successive year, meant a special bridal issue. Her article on women's lingerie through the ages fitted into this section—she was particularly dwelling on what brides had worn, and the art department had come up with some delightful sketches of bridal lingerie of the past. There would be photographs too; some of them, Lauren felt, funny rather than glamorous. Women from earlier times had worn some quite extraordinary and quite ugly garments.

Lauren had found the first year on the magazine new and exciting, but she recognised recycled articles this year—the same subject handled the same way, if written slightly differently, perhaps by a different writer. Her first enthusiasm had waned as habit took over; she wanted to move on, to one of the Cornwell newspapers, and had begun to apply whenever a suitable job was advertised internally. Cornwell staff were always given a chance to apply for a job before an advertisement was placed in the trade papers. It was easier on the management if they could fill a vacancy with someone they already employed, rather than bring in outsiders, and beside each lift on every floor of the building was a large board which always carried cards advertising any jobs available.

So far she hadn't had any luck with her applications, but one day she would hit on the right job at the right time, she was sure of that. She was ambitious, and she believed in herself. She wanted to move upward in her profession, and she wanted to do it on her own talent. She would never want Rob or his family to help her get jobs. Lauren had a tough integrity of her own. That was why she continued to work hard on *Ultra*, in spite of losing her enthusiasm for the magazine itself. This was the job she was paid to do, so Lauren worked at it.

It took her three-quarters of an hour to complete, and revise, her article, then she pressed the button that sent it whizzing off to be checked by a sub-editor before it finally went through to the printing department.

Stretching with a yawn, she got up from her desk, looking at the clock on the wall opposite. It was only half-past nine, but she felt so tired that it could have been midnight. She had been working full out all day and her mind was as dead as a flat battery.

'Going now?' asked the only other reporter still in the office. Joanne Neal was a friendly girl with a warm personality, and Lauren got on well with her, although they weren't actually close friends. Joanne was married, and too preoccupied with her home life to make friends with anyone at the magazine. Lauren guessed she wouldn't continue in her job much longer—she openly planned to have a baby and stop work before the year was out, which was why she was quite literally laid back; leaning back in her chair with her stockinged feet on her desk, her hands linked behind her head, making no pretence of doing any work.

Lauren nodded. 'At last!' She gave the dark girl a wry grin. 'Good luck with the run.' That was why Joanne was here; it was her turn to stay late, on night duty. Every print day someone had to be on hand in the office until the print run had been successfully completed, just in case last-minute changes had to be made—a very unlikely possibility, but Annie Jones was too good an editor to leave anything to chance.

She was here too, of course, in her office, but, unlike Joanne, there was no doubt Annie would be working. She loved her job.

Joanne grinned lazily. 'Thanks. Goodnight.'

Lauren reached the lifts just as one arrived. The doors opened and someone hurried out, carrying a heavy briefcase in one hand, a suitcase in the other.

Lauren automatically glanced at the tall, slim man in a slightly travel-worn suit, then her nerves jumped. 'Louis!'

He looked at her quickly and gave her a weary smile. 'Hello, Lauren. Working late? Is Annie in her office? I have to talk to her before I make tracks for home and bed.'

'Yes, Annie's here,' Lauren said, her brain in confusion. 'I...I thought you weren't due back for several days, Louis? Anything wrong?'

'Oh, I ran into some trouble over that last issue on child abuse—I told Annie it was a hot potato, and I was right.'

He was pale and irritable, and Lauren looked uneasily at him. 'You look tired—you should have gone straight home. I saw Patty across the road at the wine-bar during my supper break, and she didn't seem to be expecting you back yet. Have you let her know you'll be home tonight?'

Louis gave a groan, running a hand through his smooth dark brown hair. 'I meant to, but I was in such a rush to get the plane that I forgot! I'll ring her when I've talked to Annie.' He walked away down the corridor towards the editor's office, and Lauren watched him, her forehead creased.

Once Louis was out of sight she dashed back into the long editorial office and picked up a phone. Joanne, at the other end of the room, stared. 'Forgotten something?' she called curiously, and Lauren nodded, forcing a smile.

She leafed through her address book with one hand in search of Patty's number, then tapped it into the phone. The ringing started, then cut off, but even as Lauren opened her mouth to start speaking she heard Patty's voice say cheerfully: 'This is Patty Saville. I'm out at present, but I should be back soon, so if you'd like to leave a message...'

Lauren swore softly, slamming the phone down again. An answering machine. She stared out of the window at the night sky, the lighted windows all around this building, the sulphurous glow of street lighting.

If Patty still had her answering machine switched on, that meant she was otherwise occupied, and Lauren knew with whom, and how they were occupying themselves.

Her mouth tightened angrily, her green eyes violent. Damn Sam Hardy! Now what did she do? She was half tempted to let the worst happen, let Sam Hardy get what he deserved, and Patty too. Louis might well kill them both, and Lauren wouldn't cry if he did; served them both right.

She liked Louis a lot; he was a good man, and a nice one. He worked hard and he cared very much for his wife. Patty was much younger; there were a good ten years between them. Louis had been married once before, when he was just twenty-three, and that marriage had ended badly too. His first wife had left him for another man, and now it seemed fate was repeating the pattern. Lauren slowly walked out of the office and into the waiting lift, and still hadn't made up her mind what she ought to do when the lift reached the ground floor.

The break-up of his first marriage had hurt Louis badly. Office gossip said that it had been five years before he had even dated anyone else. Patty had had to work hard to make him notice her when she joined *Ultra*, she had once confided to Lauren. Louis had been offhand with every woman he met—he didn't trust women any more, and who could blame him?

But Patty had got through his defences because she was persistent and determined, for one thing, and for another because she was very different from his wife, who had been a curvy, sexy redhead. Patty was so tiny and sweet; a china doll of a girl with those big eyes and that delicate face and her light, whispering, childlike voice.

Patty had loved Louis once—what had gone wrong? Would she want their marriage to end? Was it Sam Hardy she wanted now? It was so hard to read another woman's mind—Lauren didn't really understand Patty at all.

She hesitated outside the building, on the pavement, then made up her mind and hailed a passing taxi. She had very little option, did she? She couldn't let Louis go home to find his wife in bed with Sam Hardy. She would have to take a taxi over to Patty's flat in Knightsbridge and warn them.

CHAPTER TWO

THE flat was on the second floor of a modern luxury apartment block, set among billiard-table-smooth green lawns, not far from Harrods. This was expensive territory, Lauren thought wryly, getting out of her taxi and handing the driver his money.

On her salary, she couldn't possibly afford to live in a place like this. Lucky Patty! But then it wasn't Patty's earning capacity that dictated where she and Louis lived. Louis earned far more than his wife; he was a highly paid executive of a large company. He would have no problem paying for one of these flats. Maybe he had lived here even before he met Patty, and they had just stayed on after their marriage?

She paused in the hallway of the building to study the numbers on the front doors, then raced up the wide flight of stairs.

Lauren's adrenalin was running high. She had to get there before Louis did, although why it should be her job to save Patty's marriage she didn't stop to ask herself.

Flushed and out of breath, she skated a look from one elegant dark green front door, gleaming with polished brass fittings, to another. Come on, come on, she thought frantically—which one is number nine?

It would be the last door she looked at, of course, tucked away in an angle of the landing. Lauren gave a sigh of relief and jammed her thumb down on to the bell. She heard the ringing start inside the flat, go on and on and on. At first there was no sign of life; no sound, no movement, then as the ringing continued she heard a door open somewhere in the flat, heard a deep, familiar voice.

She stiffened. Until that moment she had been telling herself that she could be quite wrong—Patty could be here alone. In which case she was going to look pretty silly, but she wouldn't have minded that.

Now, though, she knew for certain. Sam Hardy *was* with Patty, had been here ever since they got back from the wine-bar, and if they tried to lie to her, tried to pretend they had just been playing cards or watching TV together, she would scream.

She kept her thumb on the bell and, through the insistent ringing, heard Patty's voice, anxious and agitated.

'No, Sam, you can't go. You mustn't! I'll go, it could be a neighbour, and I don't want anyone to see you here.'

'Don't bother to answer it at all, then,' Sam said impatiently.

'I must see who it is, Sam! It could be important.'

'Just someone being nosy!' muttered Sam. 'Oh, well, do what you like.'

There was the slam of a door somewhere in the flat, then movement, rustling, footsteps.

'Who is it?' Patty asked uncertainly through the door, but Lauren didn't answer, she just kept her thumb on the bell.

'Oh, for heaven's sake, stop ringing, please!' Patty said crossly, then the front door was pulled open and she stood there, pink and dishevelled, in a long, silver-embroidered black caftan, her lipstick smudged, her dark hair ruffled, her brown eyes wide and startled as they gazed at Lauren incredulously.

Lauren had meant to deliver her message rapidly and go, but she hadn't bargained for her own temper.

One look at Patty and she knew what had been happening in that flat. Her mind filled up with images that made her sick; Patty in Sam's arms, kissing him, lying in bed with him; Sam undressing her, touching her body, taking her.

It was one thing to suspect, another to see and know for sure. Lauren went dark red with anger and distaste, for a second forgetting why she was here, although she was thinking about Louis all the time, a feverish pain throbbing inside her. How could they do this to him? He wasn't a sexy, dynamic character, but Louis was a man you could trust, a man you could always rely on, and he deserved a better wife. Patty hadn't been married to him very long; hadn't her marriage vows meant anything to her?

It was Patty who recovered first. Turning an angry red, she burst out furiously, 'Lauren! Oh, this is too much! What do you think you're doing here? Have

you followed me home to start lecturing me all over
again?'

Just as angry, Lauren said, 'No, I haven't, not that
you don't need a few home truths, Patty, but that's not
why I came. I——'

'I'm not listening! Go away!' snapped Patty, starting to shut the door.

'Don't be a fool!' Lauren put her shoulder in the
way and leant heavily on the door, forcing it back in
spite of the struggle Patty put up against her.

'Lauren, stop it!' Patty had to give up the fight, let
the door swing open again, and she was even angrier,
although her brown eyes took on a baffled look.
'What on earth has got into you? Why are you doing
this?'

'What's all this noise about?' a voice drawled behind them, and both women turned to stare as Sam
Hardy strolled along the flat hallway, calmly knotting his dark blue silk tie with one hand. He was fully
dressed; he must have thrown his clothes on in a tearing hurry, but it didn't show. Whatever he wore looked
good on him; he had a long, lean, elegant body which
moved with grace and conferred on the most casual
old clothes an air of chic.

Lauren looked contemptuously at him, though. If
he thought that that bland expression fooled her for an
instant, he was very wrong. Any other man in this situation would look confused or guilty, but not Sam
Hardy. He had no conscience, no moral sense.

His brows rose. 'Well, well, well, it's Lauren again!'
he said, his tone derisive. 'You never give up, do you?'

'She's trying to force her way in here!' Patty said indignantly. 'I told her to go away, that I didn't want any more of her good advice, but she wouldn't let me close the door.'

Sam ran a hand over his thick black hair, studying Lauren with an odd expression. 'You know, the way you're acting, anyone would think you were jealous!'

Lauren stiffened, her face burning with rage. 'Jealous!' she spat out. 'Over you? Don't flatter yourself!'

Patty took a surprised breath, eyes widening. 'Good grief—you've hit the nail on the head, Sam! Look at her face! That's what this is all about. She's jealous, she fancies you herself!'

Then she started to laugh, and Lauren felt her throat tighten with dislike so strong that it was like hatred. Patty had always been a friend, but at that moment she wanted to hit her, to yell back at her. She didn't because her anger helped her; her mind suddenly went icy cold. She had come here to deliver a warning, and she would do just that, but now she used it like a weapon, hoping it would hurt.

Tersely, she bit out, 'Louis is back.'

She had her wish. Patty stopped laughing and went white. Sam's hard grey eyes narrowed. Neither of them said anything for a moment, then Patty whispered, 'What did you say?'

'Louis is back,' repeated Lauren. 'He flew down from Glasgow this evening; I just saw him, in the office.'

'I don't believe you!' said Patty, but she did—her eyes were frightened. They turned to Sam imploringly. 'She must be lying, mustn't she? He wouldn't come home without telling me he was coming—he always calls to tell me which plane he's getting!'

Sam was watching Lauren, his black brows drawn. 'Why didn't you phone? Why come over here? It must have taken you a good quarter of an hour to drive here from the office.'

She met his eyes coldly. 'I tried to phone—all I gc was the answering machine.'

'Oh!' wailed Patty, putting her hands to her face. 'I've always hated that damned machine! Louis insisted on buying it, and showed me how to use it. I wish I hadn't set it, but I didn't want anyone ringing up while...' She broke off, biting her lip with a look at Lauren, whose face was cold and set. 'I wish I'd never touched the machine,' Patty muttered, close to tears.

Lauren looked at her, frowning, still angry, and yet sorry for her too. She had gone to pieces now, as might have been expected. That was Patty's style. Sensitive, fragile, she had always found someone stronger to help her fight her battles, usually a man. This time it would be Sam Hardy's turn to solve Patty's problem for her, and good luck to him. If Louis found him here, Sam might well find himself handling Patty's problems permanently. Patty was the marrying kind, even if she wasn't the faithful kind. She would expect him to be there if Louis divorced her.

'Well,' Lauren said brusquely, 'I have to get home. I'm tired, I've had a long day.' Her angry eyes said that her day hadn't been made any easier by having to come all this way to warn Patty that her husband was home unexpectedly, and she resented being accused of lying. 'Believe me or not, Patty, it's up to you, but Louis isn't far behind me—he just stopped off at the office because he had to talk to Annie urgently, then he was coming home. You'd better make up your mind whether or not you want to lose him—and do it fast, because you may not get a second chance.'

She turned away without even looking at either of them again, and ran down the stairs, and into the street. She would have to walk into the main road to pick up a taxi, but it would be no hardship, although she wasn't wearing a coat and her suit was made of a lightweight jersey which wasn't intended to keep out the cold. It was a clear, starlit night and the air was cool and sweet. She didn't mind the slight chill.

She began to walk quickly and had almost reached the corner when she heard footsteps behind her.

A little shiver ran down her back. She didn't look round; she didn't need to—she knew who it was, and walked faster, hoping to be able to hail a taxi before he caught up with her. She would have liked to break into a run, but she wasn't giving him the satisfaction of watching her run away from him.

He would either think she was scared of him, or, even worse, attracted to him, and he wouldn't scruple to take advantage of her if he thought he could. With a man like Sam Hardy it was wisest never to let him

think he got to you at all, in any way. You had to keep
your head and stay cool and never let him get a step
too close.

She had almost made the mistake of falling in love
with him once; it had been touch and go for a while
until she realised that an affair with Sam never lasted
long. He would get bored with her, and one day he
would regretfully make excuses and vanish. He always had, in the past, she had been told. London was
littered with Sam's discarded women.

Her informant had been a girl she met at a party; a
lively girl with short, curly fair hair and a ready smile.
Annette Simmons, remembered Lauren with a grim
smile.

She had come up to Lauren because she had spotted her with Sam earlier. He had had to leave the
party, because he was working night shift then, but
Lauren had stayed, and while she was getting herself
a plate of crisp salad Annette had joined her and introduced herself. She was a secretary in TV now, but
she had once worked on a Cornwell paper, which was
how she had got to know Sam.

'I hear you're Sam's latest! How long has it been
going on?' Annette had asked cheerfully. 'I used to
date him myself once, a few years ago.'

Lauren had been wary, then, of course, wondering
if Annette was jealous of the woman in Sam's life, and
maybe her eyes had betrayed her because Annette had
grinned and waved a hand at her, indicating the wed-
ding-ring she wore.

'Don't worry, it's all water under the bridge—I'm married to a super guy and very happy. I got over Sam a long time ago. Oh, and he was fun, while it lasted.' Her eyes had had a dreamy, nostalgic gleam, and Lauren had felt a sting of jealousy, wondering what the other girl was remembering. Then Annette had given her one of those friendly grins and shrugged. 'Oh, I have no complaints, believe me. I'm still fond of Sam, although when he first dumped me I wanted to kill him. That's how all the others feel too. Not one of them bears him a grudge.'

Lauren must have looked dumbstruck, because Annette had given her a concerned stare and asked, 'Are you OK? You look a little pale.'

Lauren had moistened her lips and repeated, '*All* the others? What others? How many others are there?'

Annette had considered her for a moment, her head to one side, looking uncertain, then said, 'I thought by now everybody knew Sam was the travelling kind? Hasn't anybody warned you about that? He never stays with one woman for long. A few months at most, usually.' She had given Lauren's white face another quick, anxious look, and begun to babble. 'But maybe this time is different . . . he has to settle down one day, and I could tell he really liked you. You looked great together, you made a lovely couple. Oh, don't take any notice of me, I talk too much, and Jim, my husband, says I never make much sense.'

Lauren hadn't answered; she had been too stunned. But although her face was stiff and white, her brain had started working. She had been thinking hard; remembering one or two girls on Sam's newspaper who had given her odd looks, had made what even at the time she had thought of as strange remarks. She had written that off as the jealousy of girls who fancied Sam themselves, but now she had seen it could have a very different meaning.

'Give me some names,' she had told Annette. 'How do I know you're telling the truth? Tell me who else he's dated?'

The other girl had been uneasy and reluctant, but in the end she had said, 'I tell you what, meet me for a drink tomorrow night, and I'll introduce you to a couple of Sam's old girlfriends. You'll see—they really like him. Faithful he isn't, but he's a nice guy, and they aren't bitter. He's just that way—some men are; they can't be faithful to one woman. And don't forget, Sam's never in one place for long. His job takes him all over the world, and sometimes he's away for months on end. His affairs just have to fit in with his way of life. He isn't the marrying kind, or it would have to be a very special woman, who didn't mind him being away so much.'

'Women marry sailors,' Lauren had said, and Annette had hurriedly agreed.

'Of course they do! And maybe Sam has got to the age when he wants to settle down, have a real home, children . . .' She had given Lauren a placatory, soothing smile. 'Look, I'm sorry about this—I wish I'd kept my mouth shut, but I really thought you must know all about him.'

Lauren had shrugged. 'That's OK,' she had said, but she had still had doubts about Annette, naturally. Annette might be telling the truth, but didn't she want to hit back at Sam too? Lauren had told herself all the next day that she wasn't going to meet her, and didn't want to hear any more about Sam's past, but in the end she had gone, and met three other young women, all of whom worked for the Cornwell organisation.

She had been curious about them; she saw that they were curious about her, but they weren't bitter or vengeful; Annette was right about that. Lauren had sat there in numb silence while they wryly swapped anecdotes about Sam.

They were all very attractive—Sam had good taste in women. They were also nice; she had liked them, been absolutely certain none of them was lying or being bitchy to spite Sam. On the contrary, they had seemed now to find his wandering habits rather endearing—almost, Lauren had felt, they boasted about him, what a wicked feller he was, you couldn't trust him out of your sight, and even then he was capable of seducing your best friend right under your nose and you none the wiser.

'Oh, but he doesn't cheat!' one of them had protested. 'He may walk out one day and never come back, but he tells you he's going, and he doesn't lie to you. At the time I hated him for being so brutally honest—he said he was sorry, but he'd fallen for someone new and it was over, then he kissed me and bought me a bracelet, and I didn't see him again for a year.' She smiled reminiscently. 'When I did, he was just as nice as ever, but by then I'd got over him, there was someone else in my life, and Sam seemed genuinely pleased to hear about him. I really like him, you know, even if he is a faithless bastard.'

'That was more or less how it happened with me,' Annette had said. 'And you're right—he doesn't cheat on his current lady, he just gets tired of her and goes off with someone new, but he's always very up front about it.'

'He's the sexiest man I ever met, anyway, and it was terrific while it lasted!' the third girl had said frankly, and they had all giggled, but Lauren had been miserable, listening to them and seeing her own fate written in their memories.

She and Sam had only been seeing each other a very short time; she wasn't yet in love with him, merely wavering on the brink, and now it had seemed that if she let herself fall in love with Sam she was doomed to be bitterly unhappy one day.

It would be her turn, next, to watch Sam walking out of her life, and there would be nothing she could do about it. Except, she had thought bleakly, never to fall in love, never let him matter—then he couldn't hurt her, could he? But if she went on seeing him, how could she stop herself caring?

There had only been one logical conclusion—she must walk away from Sam before Sam walked away from her.

She had had plenty of leave owing, so she had taken a fortnight's holiday to stay with her parents, without telling Sam where she was going, except to send him a note the night she left, to say she couldn't keep a date they had had because she had had to go away to visit a relative. She hadn't sent him any postcards, or phoned him, and when she got back she had been cool and distant; she had turned down dates, hadn't returned calls, went out publicly with other men.

She had expected Sam to be a little surprised at first, but then to shrug it off, the way all his women had shrugged him off eventually—but he had surprised her. He was angry. Only later did it dawn on her that she should have anticipated that—after all, his ego had been damaged. Until then it had always been Sam who ended an affair, never the woman. He was discovering how it felt to be dumped, and he didn't like it.

He had confronted her at her flat one Saturday morning when neither of them was working. She had opened the door expecting it to be the milkman calling for his weekly money and had found herself facing a harsh adversary.

It had been a brief interview, and a tough one. 'What's going on?' he had asked her fiercely. 'What's wrong? Why are you doing this?'

She had had a brief flash of madness when she wondered if he really cared for her, if she was making a mistake—then she had remembered those other girls, their memories of him, and the pain he had given them. Oh, they had got over it, they had all said they liked him, but Lauren didn't want to suffer the way they had.

She had looked at Sam and told him quietly what he had told so many others. 'I'm sorry; there's someone else.'

'Who?' The word had ricocheted sharply, and she had lifted her head, given him a direct, calm stare.

'Does it matter who? I'm sorry, Sam, but I don't want to see you any more—that's all that matters. Please don't make it hard for either of us, just accept it.'

He had stood there in silence, his hard grey eyes fixed on her face, and then he had turned and walked away, and she hadn't seen him again for several years.

He had been abroad a good deal, she had been busy at work, and as the time went by the whole episode had faded into the background. There had been other men she liked—not perhaps as much—and none of them had been quite right for her. She had always found a flaw somewhere; she had always stopped seeing them after a while. It wasn't until she had met Rob Cornwell that she found someone really special, and oddly enough it had been around that time that Sam came back to London permanently, after being shot by sniper fire.

She had met him again almost at once, intending to be friendly towards him, but one look and she had known they could only be enemies. No friendship was possible between the two of them, just a watchful hostility, and tonight she knew that that had flared into open warfare.

The footsteps behind her were very close now, and every muscle in her body tensed. She didn't look round, her eyes fixed on the mass of traffic moving along the high road, watching for an unoccupied taxi, but her real attention given to the man catching up with her. She knew he was angry, and she was disturbed. Sam in a temper wasn't the easiest of companions.

'Did you enjoy that?' his deep voice suddenly lashed at her, and she stiffened as he fell into step beside her, but she refused to look at him.

'Leave me alone, Sam, will you?'

He laughed shortly. 'Not yet! You're always telling people what you think of them—now it's your turn to listen. How could you talk to Patty that way, sitting in judgement on her, condemning her without knowing what you're talking about? She was already unhappy enough—now you've made her feel worse. I hope you're pleased with yourself for doing that to her. How does it feel to be so morally righteous, up there on your pedestal, looking down on everyone else?'

His tone was bitingly sarcastic, and Lauren's face burned with resentment. 'Don't try to justify yourself by attacking me!'

'Justify myself!' he exploded, grabbing her elbow and swinging her round to face him. 'I don't need to justify myself to you. All I did tonight was date an attractive woman——'

'Who happens to be married!' sneered Lauren, and he glared at her.

'That's her business, not yours—or mine, come to that!'

'Doesn't it bother you that you might have broken up a happy marriage?' Lauren's green eyes flashed up at him, contempt in them, and his mouth hardened.

'I haven't done anything of the kind. Look, you seem to think I'm having an affair with Patty. I'm not. We hadn't dated before. We just happened to run into each other in the wine-bar. I was eating a quick meal after work, and she came over to my table and asked if I'd mind if she joined me. I was glad of the company, I'd had a hard day and I was tired, and Patty is amusing and very attractive, and I like the company of women——'

'Yes,' Lauren couldn't help saying, her tone dry, and Sam gave her a grim look.

'I wasn't talking about sex. There are other reasons for liking women, you know!'

Lauren laughed angrily. 'Go on, tell me some of your best friends are women,' she mocked, and he eyed her with dislike.

'As it happens, yes. But you, lady, are not one of them! I don't remember ever disliking anyone as much as I dislike you!'

'Well, thank you for that!' she bit back, but she felt a sting of rejection inside her, although she didn't want Sam to like her, or be her friend. She didn't want Sam Hardy within a mile of her, if she could help it, but stupidly it hurt to hear him say he didn't like her. It was contrary and contradictory of her to feel that way, but she couldn't help her feelings.

Curtly, Sam said, 'You're going to listen to this, whether you like it or not!' He was gripping both her arms and bending towards her with those angry eyes fixed on her face. 'Patty and I shared a meal and talked, and I got the impression she was lonely and not too happy. Then you turned up with your rich boyfriend, looking shocked, and gave Patty a lecture about being faithful to Louis, and being sensible, and I think that pushed her into inviting me back to her place, so in a way it's as much your fault as anyone's.'

'Oh, it's my fault now, is it?' Lauren said furiously. 'I might have known it would be!'

'You put the idea into her head!'

'It was there before either of you even saw me!' Lauren snapped. 'I was watching you from the other side of the bar...'

'Oh, you were watching me, were you?' he interrupted, and suddenly the atmosphere was different between them. Sam's eyes had narrowed and were probing her face in speculation, and Lauren felt herself go pink.

Breathlessly, she said, 'Patty—I was watching Patty.' She couldn't meet his eyes and looked away just in time to glimpse an empty taxi coming towards them. 'Oh, a taxi!' she said, and Sam turned, letting go of her.

She leapt forward, waving an arm wildly, but the driver ignored her and was sailing past when Sam let out a piercing whistle. The taxi screeched to a halt like an obedient dog.

'Goodnight,' Lauren muttered to Sam, reaching for the door, but he had got there first and was opening it.

He took her arm and pushed her into the back, climbing in after her and giving the driver her address.

Lauren couldn't bear to make a scene in front of the taxi-driver, so she sat back in the corner of the back seat, staring out of the window without looking at Sam, her profile rigid.

Quietly he said, 'After we took that taxi from the wine-bar, I intended to drop Patty at her flat and go on home myself, but she asked me in for coffee.

Lauren laughed grimly. 'Coffee? Is that the buzz word for it these days?'

He was getting angrier, his voice deep and rough. 'Patty needed to talk, she needed company.'

'You didn't make love to her?' she shot back, and he scowled.

'That's not your business. I certainly didn't do anything Patty didn't invite me to do!'

Lauren eyed him contemptuously. 'I'm sure she'd love to hear you put all the blame on her!'

An angry dark red crawled up his face and his grey eyes glittered. 'You really are a bitch, aren't you? OK, if you want to blame me, go ahead. I can't stop you.'

'Thanks!' she snapped. 'I was going to!'

She felt his body tighten with rage, and for an instant she even thought he might be going to hit her, but then he drew a harsh breath and said, 'Doesn't it occur to you that if Patty was happy with Louis she wouldn't be dating other men?'

'That may be so, but it's Louis she should be talking to, not you!'

'That's what I told her,' he said curtly.

'Did you tell her that before you made love to her, or afterwards?' Lauren asked, and Sam swore under his breath.

Then the taxi turned a corner at some speed, almost collided with something coming the other way and skidded wildly, throwing Lauren sideways against Sam, who instinctively grabbed her, his arm going round her. It was such a shock that for a second she couldn't see or hear, couldn't even breathe; then she broke out of it, and away from him, sitting upright, pushing his hand down, her pulse running away from her and her breathing ragged.

She was afraid to look at Sam, afraid of what might show in her face. She was shaken to her depths by how she had just felt. She didn't even like the man; why had she gone into a witless panic simply because she had fallen against him in a taxi?

Sam was silent too, which worried her even more. What was he thinking? Was he watching her? She dared not risk looking at him in case he was, so she didn't even know if he realised what his touch had done to her.

It seemed an endless moment before Sam said quietly, 'As I was saying, Patty's marriage has run into a problem. You might talk to her about it yourself, if she'll talk to you after tonight. She badly needs to talk to someone who's sympathetic and will take the time to listen. You used to be her friend. If you really care about her, try to help. I don't know exactly what's wrong between them, whether it's just that Louis is too busy or always away, or if there's another woman—it wasn't really very clear what Patty thought, but she was very upset, there's no doubt about that. She's at the end of her tether.'

Lauren had to respect the grave note in his voice; he wasn't just making excuses, he was concerned about Patty.

'I'll try to talk to her tomorrow,' she said slowly. 'If, as you say, she's speaking to me!'

'Could you blame her if she isn't? You must have made her feel even worse. You have a blistering turn of phrase when you like.'

'I have a lot of time for Louis Saville; he's a man I trust and respect,' Lauren said and Sam laughed angrily.

'Feelings you don't have for me, I gather? What exactly is it you do feel about me, Lauren?'

She stiffened, not looking at him, and then to her relief the taxi turned into the road where she lived. She couldn't wait to get away from Sam, he had given her a disturbing shock a few minutes ago, and she was afraid he knew it. What else did his question mean? But she wasn't answering him—she couldn't. She needed to be alone, to think, to work out what had happened to her when his arm went around her. It had felt like an electric shock—it had been as violent as that—and it had left her shaking and scared.

Somehow, though, she had to throw Sam off the scent. If he so much as suspected that she might fancy him, he wouldn't rest until he had got her into bed. She had damaged his ego when she walked out on him last time, and Sam Hardy was the sort of man to think revenge was sweet.

'I think you're right; Patty must be at the end of her tether,' she said coolly, as the taxi pulled up outside her apartment block. 'Any woman who picks you up has to be pretty desperate,' and then she dived out without looking at him, handed the driver the amount which showed on the meter, and ran, half afraid that Sam might get out of the taxi and follow her. He didn't.

CHAPTER THREE

A WEEK later, Lauren came out of the lift on her floor of the Cornwell building and paused to look at the bulletin board which carried all the internal advertisements for jobs currently available. She had enjoyed her time on *Ultra*, but she had done everything she could there and she wanted to move on to something new. Her eyes flicked rapidly over the cards pinned on the board, then she sighed and turned to walk away.

'Still looking for a new job?' The dry voice of her editor made her start and turn her head with a quick smile.

'Oh, hello, Annie.' She had made no secret of her desire to move on some day, so she didn't feel guilty, although Annie was frowning. Lauren smiled frankly at the other woman. 'Yes, but there's nothing interesting available at the moment.'

'You know, I don't like to feel you're doing your job here with one eye permanently on the horizon!' Annie walked on down the corridor, a tall, slender, elegant woman in her late thirties who had a profile like Nefertiti and the physical stamina of an Olympic athlete. She could work non-stop day and night as the monthly deadline approached, without showing signs of fatigue, and she never seemed to lose her vibrant enthusiasm for the magazine, the job she did.

'I give my job a hundred per cent!' Lauren kept pace with her, frowning.

'I should hope you do! I can always get someone else to do your job, remember, Lauren.'

Lauren was taken aback, and looked sideways at that starkly lovely profile. 'Is something wrong, Annie? The bulletin board is there so that members of staff can apply for other jobs—everyone always has done, so why are you angry with me for doing it?'

'I'd like a little loyalty once in a while!' Annie snapped, a flush on her high cheekbones. She had smooth black hair which she wore cut short, in a masculine style that emphasised the beauty of her features and her faintly almond-shaped black eyes.

'That's very unfair, if you're implying that I'm disloyal!' Lauren protested in dismay, following Annie into her office and closing the door so that Annie's secretary, Jill, should not hear what was being said. Not that Jill would spread it around the office; she wouldn't keep her job long if she was a gossip, but Jill did have a passion for knowing everything that went on, was always eavesdropping, and was not above snooping through people's files to find out more about them which she would softly hint at from time to time but in a way that made it hard to pin her down.

Walking over to her desk, Annie sat down behind it, her hands on her desk and her eyes lowered. 'Oh, sit down, Lauren!' she said brusquely, and Lauren sat in the chair opposite, watching her.

Annie was sometimes a difficult woman, tough and demanding, but she was also a brilliant editor; inventive, quick, stimulating and with a great gift for organisation. If Annie had a fault it was a one-track mind. For her the only job worth having was working on *Ultra*; she couldn't understand why anyone should want to leave. Lauren was well aware that Annie's life began and ended here, in this building. Annie had founded *Ultra*, was its first and so far only editor, and didn't hide her deep pride in the magazine which was her brain-child.

'What's wrong, Annie?' Lauren asked tentatively, sure that something was bothering the other woman.

Looking up, Annie sighed and shrugged her narrow shoulders in the black silk shirt she wore so strikingly with a smooth-fitting white wool skirt.

'I've had an offer,' she said slowly, and Lauren stared, not surprised by that news. She knew Annie often got offers of other jobs from rivals of the Cornwell family, eager to snatch away their top editor.

'What's new about that?'

Annie smiled a wryly graceful acceptance of the implied compliment. 'This time it's from Charlie,' she said, and Lauren blinked.

'Charlie?'

'Cornwell.'

That was shock news all right. 'Charlie Cornwell made you an offer? What sort of offer?' asked Lauren in a puzzled voice.

'He wants me to start a new magazine.' Annie's voice was light and controlled, but there was a little tic beating beside her mouth. Before Lauren could react, Annie went on, 'He thinks I've been editing *Ultra* long enough, it's time I moved on—he says I'm getting stale, and so is the magazine, and we both need a change.'

Sympathy in her green eyes, Lauren said, 'And you hate the idea?'

'*Ultra* is my magazine!' Annie broke out passionately, her hands clenched on top of her desk. 'He has no right to take it away from me!'

Frowning, Lauren asked slowly, 'Did he say he would, whether you agreed or not?'

'I had the feeling that he would,' Annie said with bitterness, then her head lifted and she fixed her burning dark eyes on Lauren across the desk. 'He's just making excuses, of course, when he says the magazine is stale and I'm tired—he wants to give *Ultra* to someone else, and he has to get rid of me to do it.'

Lauren sensed something was coming, but she couldn't possibly have guessed what it would be. Annie paused, staring at her fixedly, then shot the words like daggers. 'Has he offered it to you?'

Lauren's jaw dropped. 'Me?' she almost squeaked, at first imagining it was a joke, but Annie wasn't smiling; there was no humour of any kind in those angry eyes. 'No!' Lauren said, shaking her head. 'No, of course not—I'm not editor material. Not yet. I hope I will be, one day, but good heavens, Annie, I'm only twenty-six. That's far too young; they don't make someone of my age an editor.'

'They do if she's going to marry Charlie Cornwell's son,' said Annie with a cynical twist of the mouth, and then the penny dropped, and Lauren felt faintly sick as she realised why the editor had shown her such hostility lately, although at one time they had been on friendly terms.

'No,' she said, paling. 'Annie, why do you think I've been applying for other jobs? Because I'd prefer to work on a newspaper. I've enjoyed working on *Ultra*, but I've been here two years and I want to make a change, and I assure you I don't want your job. I've never had any ambitions in that direction, and anyway you've got it all wrong if you think Charlie Cornwell would do anything like that for me.'

Annie laughed shortly. 'I know Charlie Cornwell very well; don't tell me what he would or wouldn't do. Charlie's ruthless in getting what he wants, and he believes in keeping power in the hands of his family. Once you've married Rob you'll be one of the family, and he'll want you in a top job.'

'That's just it, Annie!' Lauren's green eyes were bleak. 'He doesn't want me to marry his son—he wouldn't move you to make room for me. He'd just love to get rid of me; he won't even let Rob bring me home to meet him. I've been half expecting him to tell you to fire me.'

Annie leaned back in her chair, her brows together, studying Lauren's face with searching eyes. 'I know he hasn't been too happy about it,' she frowned. 'But he hasn't said anything lately, and I thought he'd got used to the idea.'

'I don't think so!' Lauren grimaced. 'I think he's just been hoping Rob and I would quarrel and split up.'

Annie bit her lower lip thoughtfully. 'I know how ruthless Charlie can be with other people's lives! He's an arrogant man, and he's always dominated Rob. It was tough on Rob having a father like that—he's been spoilt and given anything he wanted, but he's always had to do what his father dictated. Charlie's a self-made man, and proud of it, but I think he wanted Rob to marry old money, into one of the old families. He certainly had dreams of a big society wedding.'

'Rob hinted as much. It's been made very clear to me that I'm not good enough for the son of Charlie Cornwell.' Lauren's voice quivered with hurt and anger, and she stopped talking because she couldn't trust herself to say another word or she might burst into tears.

A little silence fell, then, obsessed with her own problems and not very concerned with Lauren's, Annie thought aloud, 'But if he isn't pushing me out to make way for you, why does he want me to move on from *Ultra*?'

'Maybe he just meant exactly what he said?' suggested Lauren, and Annie made a wry face.

'Maybe, but I have the feeling that there's something behind all this!'

Her phone rang and she frowned, then picked it up. 'Yes?' Her face changed. 'Uh, hello, Charlie!' Her dark eyes flicked across the desk to Lauren's face, a smile glimmering in them. 'Yes,' she said into the phone, 'I've thought about what you said, of course.' A pause, then, 'Yes, Charlie, I've got time to come and see you. Right away? In ten minutes? I'll see you then.'

Hanging up, she smiled ironically at Lauren. 'He wants to discuss his plans for me. He hopes I've had time to think over what he said last night.' She laughed shortly. 'As if I've thought of anything else these past twelve hours! But that's typical of Charlie; he drops a bomb on you and then blandly asks if you've noticed the explosion!'

She rose to her feet, her slender body graceful in motion, and Lauren watched her, wondering why Annie had never married. She was certainly a beautiful woman, and she always seemed to have a good-looking man in tow whenever she went to a social event, but office gossip had never linked her name with that of anyone in particular, except possibly Charlie Cornwell himself from time to time, but that was only because she was so often in Charlie's company.

It made good copy for gossip columnists, of course, who preferred to think Annie had got her job through sleeping her way to the top rather than working her way up, but anyone who knew her would laugh at the idea. Annie would never have needed to compromise over anything. She hadn't climbed to the top; she had soared, effortlessly, through sheer ability.

Lauren went back to her own office and settled down to work, but she was writing a piece on a subject she had handled before several times—teenage rebellion—and although she had managed to find a new angle from which to view it she was finding it hard to find much to say about it that she had not said before, and that was a bore.

'Stop sighing!' Joanne Neal said, grinning at her from the next desk, and Lauren made a face back.

'Sorry, was I? Joanne, you've been on the magazine for a few years—how do you cope with writing about the same subjects over and over again?'

'I'm lucky; I never remember what I've written before!'

Lauren laughed. 'You're kidding?'

'No, seriously—I have a very short memory. I just do my job, go home and forget about it.' Joanne leaned back in her chair, linking her hands behind her head. 'Phil and I will have saved enough, by Christmas, for me to stop work altogether and have a baby. Phil gets a rise at the end of the year, which will easily cover the mortgage repayments and the various bills, and our savings will tide us over for quite a while, until I can get myself some freelance work to do at home.'

'Well, I hope it all works out for you just the way you plan,' Lauren said gently, and Joanne smiled at her, eyes glowing.

'Thanks. Lauren, don't take work too seriously—if you have to do an article you did last year, dig out the first one and see how you did it then, and try to make a better job of it this time. There's always room for improvement.'

Lauren grimaced wryly. 'Isn't that the truth?'

She went down to lunch in the canteen at around one o'clock, and met Louis Saville in the lift coming back up again. Lauren tightened up when she saw him, aware of all the things she wasn't telling him and couldn't tell him, and guilty because of it.

Louis was quite unaware of that, though, and gave her a friendly smile. 'Oh, Lauren! I was going to pop in to see you later; this will save me the trouble. We're having a party on Saturday night and we hope you'll come. You know where we live, don't you?'

'Yes,' she murmured, a little flushed as she recalled her last visit there.

'Good. Eight o'clock. Bring a friend, if you like.' His eyes twinkled. 'Unless you think Rob Cornwell might find us all very low-life!'

Lauren laughed at the mild joke. 'Thank you—I'll ask Rob if he's free on Saturday night. I'm sure he'd love to come, but he has a lot of semi-official entertaining to do, as you know—for his father or the company.'

'But you'll come, with or without him?' prompted Louis, his thin figure poised for flight as he left the lift at his floor.

Lauren looked into his gentle eyes and felt a twinge of compassion for him. He was such a lovely man. His first marriage had ended tragically, and now his second one was in serious trouble—it simply wasn't fair. Louis Saville deserved to have a wonderfully happy home life; why wasn't he getting one?

'Yes, I'd love to come,' she said warmly, to make him smile, and he did.

'Good, look forward to seeing you, Lauren. You're good for Patty; I wish she saw more of you—a pity she ever left *Ultra*.' He stopped short, grimacing, nodded to Lauren and hurriedly walked off down the corridor.

He had almost confided in her, Lauren sensed, frowning, as she pressed the lift button and they moved on upwards. She was relieved he hadn't; the last thing she wanted was to have to listen to Louis's side of this messy situation; and as she walked to her desk she wished she hadn't said so certainly that she would go to this party. She could have told a little white lie, said she had another date, or said she would try to come and then not bothered to turn up!

She and Rob were going to a first night that evening, so she had to hurry home to change into something special for the occasion, and left the office dead on five o'clock.

Rob picked her up at six-thirty, and they had a little light supper at a West End restaurant before walking the few hundred yards to the theatre.

Over caviar, with all the usual garnishing of boiled egg, capers and chopped raw onion, served with champagne, she told Rob about the party the Savilles were giving, and he consulted his diary.

'Yes, nothing down here—let's go, it could be fun.' His grin was wicked. 'And if they've invited Sam Hardy we could have fireworks as well!'

'Don't laugh about it!' Lauren said, frowning.

'Darling, they're all grown-ups, they play grown-up games, and sometimes someone gets hurt, but it isn't a tragedy, it's a farce. Louis isn't a fool—if he doesn't know yet that his wife is having an affair with Sam Hardy, he'll find out sooner or later, and then the sparks will fly.'

He laughed, but Lauren didn't. She was disturbed; Rob had always refused to take anything too seriously—there was a streak of dark glee in him that enjoyed watching other people fall on their faces—but Lauren had been sure that that was just on the surface; that underneath that there was another Rob, a man with deep feelings he was careful to keep hidden. She blamed Charlie Cornwell for all Rob's little human flaws. It seemed to her that the odd mix of spoiling and punishment which Charlie had handed out to Rob all his life had warped Rob's nature.

She hadn't told Rob about her clash with Sam Hardy on the night they saw him with Patty in the wine-bar, and she wondered if she should. If Sam had been telling the truth, he wasn't the cause of the trouble between Patty and Sam, and maybe she should tackle Patty some day soon, and try to find out what was wrong and maybe if she could do anything to help?

But had he been telling the truth? She had a strong feeling Rob wouldn't believe a word of it, would just laugh at her for letting Sam pull the wool over her eyes.

During the party on Saturday she would watch Patty and Sam, and perhaps get a clearer picture.

As they walked to the theatre a short time later, she asked Rob tentatively, 'Did you know your father wanted Annie to leave *Ultra*?'

Rob shot her a look. 'She told you?'

'I was there when he rang her this morning, and she mentioned that he felt she should move on.'

'Dad thinks it's a mistake to stay too long anywhere,' Rob said, shrugging.

'But *Ultra* was her personal project!' Lauren said, her voice passionate. 'She dreamt it up and has made it one of the best-selling magazines of the decade! Turning her back on all that will be like dying a little—can't he see that?'

Rob frowned, his face irritated. 'I shouldn't take sides if I were you, Lauren! My father knows what he's doing. It isn't wise to get into a wrangle with him; he won't forget it.'

Lauren paled, taken aback by the dismissive tone of his voice. 'Surely I have a right to my own opinion!'

'So long as you keep it to yourself, yes!' he snapped, and she stiffened in shock. This was a Rob she didn't know or recognise; he had never talked to her this way before, but then they had never discussed Cornwell family business tactics before. Rob had kept their relationship very personal, she realised, looking back over the months. She had assumed from his silences that he wasn't involved in the inner councils of the company, but now she wondered. Had Rob merely been careful never to offer her confidences?

Rob was watching her sideways, his mouth wry. He suddenly slid an arm around her waist and pulled her closer as they halted outside the theatre. 'Darling, don't look like that! Did I snarl at you?' His voice was coaxing, placatory, as he smiled down at her and kissed her lightly. 'I'm sorry, angel face. It's just that I badly want you and my father to get on, remember. If we're ever going to get round him, he must be sure you'll be on his side, and really he does know what he's talking about, in the newspaper business. He ought to. He's been in it long enough, since he was just a kid of fourteen, selling papers on a street corner! He's only preaching what he's practised himself over forty years in the trade. He says you either grow or you stagnate—nothing stays the same for ever, and it's madness to try to stand still.'

Lauren had to admit that that made some sense, and sighed, nodding. 'I suppose there's something in that.'

Rob grinned. 'There you are! Once you look at it from his point of view, he's usually right. He thinks Annie Jones is going stale; he thinks she needs a new challenge to stimulate her. Dad thinks the world of her, you know. He wouldn't do anything to upset her if he could help it, and the last thing he wants is for her to leave, so in the end he'll let Annie make the decision herself, but I think she'll soon see things his way, once she's thought about it.' He looked down at Lauren, his eyes warm. 'Just as you did, darling.'

Lauren smiled back, but inside she felt oddly chilled. Did Rob always see things from his father's point of view, once he had had time to think about them? Was that what Charlie Cornwell was waiting for, where his son and Lauren were concerned?

Was he refusing to meet her, or accept her relationship with his son, because he was waiting for Rob to come round to his point of view?

All that evening, while she watched a play everyone around her seemed to find hilarious, she was muted and unable to laugh. She was wondering how long it would take for Rob to realise that, as always, it seemed, his father was right, about her as about everything else.

For the rest of that week she didn't see Rob, because he had been sent over to Paris by his father on business for a couple of days.

'I'd love to take you with me, darling!' he said on the phone the night before he went, and Lauren's eyes lit up.

'Oh, I'd love to go too!'

Quickly, Rob said, 'But I'm afraid it's impossible—I'm going with a team of others, all accountants! You'd be bored out of your skull, because I wouldn't see anything of you—I'll be totally involved, twelve hours a day, with these discussions. It isn't even interesting business. I wish it was!'

Lauren had suppressed disappointment. 'Never mind—I understand. You will be back for the party on Saturday night, won't you?'

'Wouldn't miss it for worlds!' Rob said lightheartedly. 'I want a ringside seat in case Louis Saville punches Sam Hardy on the nose.'

Lauren hung up, frowning. Sometimes she almost didn't like Rob, but then the way men's minds worked often baffled her. They seemed to have such very different ideas of humour. She couldn't believe he meant what he had said; he was just joking. Not a very funny joke, but not maliciously intended, surely?

When Rob got back from Paris on the following Saturday afternoon, he rang her and arranged to pick her up that evening at seven.

'Should we have dinner first, or will there be food?'

'Louis says they'll serve a light buffet supper at around ten.'

'I shall be starving to death by then,' said Rob. 'Let's eat before we go, OK? I'll book a table at that Italian place around the corner from your flat.'

They only had Escalope Milanese, served with red Italian wine, and then coffee, but it was half-past eight when they arrived at the party.

'We were just deciding that you weren't coming,' Louis reproached them.

'Are we the last?' Rob threw a quick look around, but there was no sign of Sam Hardy in the crowded room.

'A few people haven't turned up yet,' Louis agreed.

'No Sam Hardy?' Rob asked, and Lauren tensed, sliding her hand up his arm and pinching him in warning. He grinned sideways at her, shaking his head, meaning that he wouldn't drop any heavy hints, but Louis was blissfully unaware of any undercurrents.

He was smiling cheerfully. 'Sam will be late, he's had a big photo session down at Leeds Castle—a conference of television producers from America, I think he said. He'll be along in an hour or so. Now, how about a drink, you two? Lauren, you look quite lovely, doesn't she, Rob?'

Rob looked at her, his eyes warm. 'She looks beautiful!'

Lauren smiled at them both. 'Flatterers!' All the same, she knew she was looking her best. She was wearing a long, clinging white silk dress with a deep neckline; it moulded itself softly to her breasts, hips, thighs, flowing as she moved, and the gleam of it gave her blonde hair a richer gold, made her green eyes glisten mysteriously. It had cost a fortune, but because it was a classic style and beautifully cut it would never be out of fashion; so long as it fitted her she would be able to go on wearing it.

She and Rob took a glass each and moved on into the throng of people, most of whom they knew. Patty was with a group nearby; she and Lauren looked warily at each other, then Lauren smiled coaxingly and blew her a silent kiss and Patty laughed, slackening. They had known each other too long for a spat over Sam Hardy to make them enemies.

The flat wasn't really big enough for the number of guests at the party; it was rather like playing Sardines for a while, elbowing your way through shouting groups, leaning against walls to stay upright—but after an hour or so some people who had long journeys home ahead of them left, and there was a little more space between everyone, so Patty and Louis served the supper buffet, which turned out to be finger food; easy to eat without a knife or fork on a paper plate.

Lauren perched on a windowsill and Rob leaned against her knees while she fed him, as if he were a child, his teeth nibbling her fingertips as she pushed tiny pieces of quiche into his mouth. He laughed backwards at her and she kissed the top of his head, and then above him, and across the room, her eyes met the derisive gaze of Sam Hardy, who had just walked in and was standing by the door.

Lauren felt an electric jolt, every one of her nerve-ends seeming to jerk in recoil. Flushed and furious with herself for that reaction, she quickly moved her eyes on to a girl standing beside Sam. She had never seen her before—had she come with Sam? Or was it coincidence that they had walked in together?

'Wow!' Rob said at that moment, and glancing down at him Lauren saw that he was staring at the same girl, his eyes like saucers. 'Who's *that*?'

'No idea,' Lauren said crisply, eating the last piece of quiche herself.

'Hey, she's with Sam Hardy!' Rob realised, open-mouthed. 'Cunning devil! He brought a red herring with him.'

'Redhead, you mean,' Lauren said, and Rob roared with laughter at the feeble joke. The girl's hair was red; flame-red, an extraordinary colour which was made even more amazing by her yellow-amber eyes and full, flame-red, sultry mouth. She had a sexy figure, long and slinky, and emphasised it by wearing a dress which looked as if it had been sprayed on. The material was jersey, but it had been made in a dappled, leopard-skin pattern which perfectly matched her hair and eyes and gave her the look of a jungle feline, a big cat. Even her nails were like talons, long and lethal, the same colour as her lipstick.

Lauren looked around the room and saw most of the men staring. Patty was staring too, her lower lip trembling, a sheen to her eyes, as though at any moment she might burst into tears.

'Well, you told me Sam Hardy was as fast as a snake, struck like lightning and then moved on, but I didn't realise he was this fast!' Rob said with a grin, then he caught sight of Patty's face too, and whistled softly. 'Oh, dear, somebody isn't very happy.'

'Don't be so insensitive, Rob!' Lauren muttered, sliding from the windowsill. Sometimes the way he thought grated on her. He had been spoilt as a child, that was the problem. His father's ruthless cynicism had rubbed off a little, although Rob was much warmer, more lovable.

'What did I say?' he asked blankly, and maybe she was being unfair.

'Never mind. Here, find a home for this, would you?' she said, thrusting her empty plate at him and making purposefully for Patty, but before she got to her Patty rushed away through the gossiping groups of people that filled the room, into the kitchen.

Lauren followed, and found her alone, leaning on the sink, her head bent, her body quivering. Lauren closed the door and stood there watching her for an instant, then she went over to her and put an arm round her.

'Don't cry, Patty,' she said quietly, hugging her. 'Not over Sam Hardy. He isn't worth wasting the salt water over. I warned you about what he was like, didn't I?'

Patty sniffed childishly, turning her head away. 'If you've come to say I told you so, don't,' she muttered.

'Sorry, I didn't mean to,' Lauren said, pulling some kitchen paper off the roll on the wall and pushing it into her fingers. 'Come on, wipe your eyes. I can't believe you were in love with him—it was just a game, right? And it's gone wrong, but there's no point in crying over it.'

Patty rubbed her wet eyes and face, screwed up the paper and dropped it into a bin. She gave a little sob. 'But I liked him a lot, and it made me feel better, having one man around who seemed to like me!'

Lauren felt like smacking her. Crossly she said, 'You and Sam Hardy have a lot more in common than I'd thought. You're both ruthless, and you both have inflated egos. Oh, snap out of it, Patty! You should be glad Sam has got someone else. At least Louis won't suspect anything has been going on between you two!'

'Oh! Do you think that's why Sam brought her?' Patty picked up the idea like a squirrel picking up an unexpected nut; excitedly, in a hurry.

'What difference does it make?' said Lauren, doubting it.

Patty was very attractive, but the redhead was seduction in human form, and Lauren couldn't imagine Sam Hardy passing up a temptation like that. He had decided to stay away from Patty in future, and was going public with this new affair. If Patty had any sense she would just forget about him.

'Sam's laying a false trail!' Patty thought aloud. 'Of course, I should have realised.' She sighed. 'I haven't seen him alone for days. We can't talk in the office, and after work he's a very hard man to get hold of. I've got to talk to him, though. I want to know how I stand. I really thought he…we…oh, I have to know what's going to happen—— Lauren, you see that, don't you?' She looked imploringly at her. 'Lauren, do you think you could persuade Rob to ask that girl to dance, so that I can talk to Sam alone just for a minute?'

Furious, Lauren shook her head. 'I won't do anything of the sort! Are you quite crazy? Don't you ever learn?'

'Just a few minutes, that's all I need,' Patty said desperately, and Lauren looked at her with disbelief.

'And what if Louis notices you two, and starts getting suspicious?'

'He won't, if you dance with him!'

'No, Patty!'

'I only need three minutes, Lauren!'

'Just forget the man!'

'I will, I promise—but I must make sure he realises it's all over.'

Lauren frowned, remembering Sam's insistence that no affair had ever begun. Which of them was telling the truth?

Patty clutched Lauren's arm and turned pleading eyes on her. 'Lauren, please! Just three minutes, and then I'll forget about him.'

'I must be nearly as crazy as you are!' Lauren said, weakening, and went over to talk to Rob.

He grinned from ear to ear. 'Dance with Sam Hardy's latest lady while the one before her kisses him goodbye? Well, why not? I'm always ready to sacrifice myself in a good cause!'

Eyeing him with mock-threat, Lauren snapped, 'Flirt with her, and you're a dead man!'

'I love it when you're jealous!' teased Rob, and went over to where Sam Hardy and the redhead were being besieged by admirers. Lauren watched from a distance while Rob peeled the redhead away from Sam, who gave him a cold stare. The two of them began to dance to the smoky music Louis had put on the tape deck. The crowd around Sam began to diminish once the redhead had gone, and Patty discreetly slipped over to him. Lauren turned her back; she did not want to watch the two of them together. How would Sam handle this? He must be an expert by now at saying goodbye to a woman.

A little crowd of reporters were talking near her; she picked up Sam's name and couldn't help listening. 'Trust Sam Hardy to go out on a routine photo session and come back with a raving beauty!' said a man she recognised from Sam's paper, the *Gazette*.

'Not just that,' grinned the *Gazette*'s television critic, Alan Cox. 'Her father's one of these American TV producers, Hal Earl. He's behind that new soap topping the ratings here at the moment, and this girl worked on the set herself.'

The others all listened to him with respect; Alan was never wrong about his own subject. He had amazing sources of information about anything to do with television.

'Actress?' asked someone, and Alan shook his head.

'No, an assistant director—mind you, that doesn't mean much, but with Daddy's help I expect she'll end up as a director.'

'Not only looks, but influence!' said a dark-haired girl reporter with some bitterness. 'This is not a fair world!'

'Whoever thought it was, Cornelia?' Alan mocked, and she made a face at him, then looked across the room at Sam, who was now with Patty. 'Hey, where's the American girl gone to?' she asked, surprised, and they all glanced around.

'Well, well,' drawled Tom Slade, the paper's gossip columnist, sneering slightly, 'Rob Cornwell has snatched her away! Those two should have a lot in common. Even Sam Hardy doesn't have a hope of competing with Rob. Sam doesn't have the Cornwell money behind him.'

'I thought Rob was dating a girl on Ultra?' Alan Cox said, and Lauren flushed, hurriedly retreating before they noticed her eavesdropping.

Louis appeared beside her, smiling in his calm, gentle way. 'Hello, Lauren—haven't you got a drink? Let me get you one.'

'No, thanks,' she said, forcing a smile back. 'I've had enough. What a lovely party, Louis. I hope you're enjoying it as much as the rest of us?'

'It's nice to see so many friends in one room,' Louis said, a little evasively, she felt. 'But why are you all alone? Where's Rob?' Lauren involuntarily glanced sideways, and Louis's eyes flicked from her to Rob and the redhead. He frowned, then said quickly, 'Ah, he's talking to Janice Earl—good. Her father's an old friend of Charlie Cornwell, Sam told me, so Rob's very wise to get to know her. That will please his father.' He smiled soothingly at Lauren. 'Come and talk to Patty—let me see, where is she?' He turned to look around. 'Ah, there she is, with Sam.' He took Lauren's arm and insisted on guiding her over to Patty and Sam.

Sam wore his poker face; Patty was very flushed and agitated, and Louis gave her a frowning look. 'Something wrong, darling?'

'I've been trying to persuade her to dance, but she says she's too busy playing hostess,' Sam said lightly. 'Lauren, what about you? You don't have Patty's excuse!'

Louis looked approving, so that Lauren felt she had no choice. She had to let Sam put his arm round her and move her across the floor to the music, his body touching hers. She was intensely, angrily conscious of that. It was a long time since he had held her in his arms, and she had to grit her teeth to bear it.

'I ought to slap you,' he murmured in her ear, his cheek against her hair.

She stiffened, dancing like an automaton. 'What did you say?'

'Why did you get your boyfriend to dance with Janice so that Patty could get me into a corner?' he accused, and she moved back to glare up at him.

'Patty said she just wanted to say goodbye.'

His arm tightened, pulling her back against him. She wasn't getting into a fight with him in public, but her body silently resisted, arching away from him.

'She lied to you,' Sam muttered, lowering his cheek to hers, and she grabbed hold of his arm and dug her fingers into it in a warning that she was getting angry.

'Stop touching me like that!' she whispered. 'And don't run Patty down to me! You of all people have no right to——'

'Patty's a bored and frustrated woman whose husband doesn't spend enough time with her!' Sam bit out. 'I told you the problem last time we talked about her. It's Louis she has to talk to, not me. I thought you had more sense than to give her a chance to work herself up into an emotional state at her own party. She's got it into her head that I only brought Janice as a cover so that Louis shouldn't think it was Patty I was really interested in! Whatever I say or do she can twist to mean what she wants it to mean!'

'You should never have got involved with her in the first place!' hissed Lauren. 'But you can't resist taking anything that's on offer, can you?'

A dark red crawled up his face and his eyes leapt with rage as he stared at her. 'I didn't take you,' he snarled, and Lauren went rigid, her face on fire.

'I was never on offer to you!' she whispered, aware of all the people around them.

'That's not how I remember it,' Sam said, then the arm around her waist became an iron bar, forcing her against him so that all the breath seemed to be crushed out of her. They were both fully clothed, but they might as well have been naked—Sam's movements had an intimacy that was quite deliberate; he intended to make her aware of him, and he succeeded. His thigh kept brushing hers, his arm possessively holding her waist, his long, slim body smoothly moving against her. Her skin was burning and her green eyes had a wild look to them. Sam looked down through lowered black lashes at her, his mouth curling in a mocking little smile.

'That is how I remember you,' he said softly, and Lauren couldn't bear any more. She broke away from him, her breathing fast and painful, hating those amused, cynical eyes. It was sheer luck that at that moment the tape ended and everyone else stopped dancing.

Louis hurried to the tape deck to change the music, and Lauren caught sight of Rob not far away, at the bar. He was no longer with Janice Earl. He was getting himself a drink, and he looked irritated.

'Oh, there you are!' Lauren said huskily, joining him, but still off balance after her encounter with Sam Hardy.

'Hi,' said Rob, looking round, his mouth sulky. 'I'm not speaking to you! Why did you saddle me with that vain little bitch?'

'You didn't like her?' Lauren said vaguely, conscious of Sam at a distance, watching them.

'Like her? I'll tell you what I think of her—she's been badly spoilt, and what she needs is a damn good slapping. Sam Hardy's welcome to her!'

'She's welcome to Sam Hardy!' Lauren said, without keeping her voice down, and hoped Sam had heard her.

CHAPTER FOUR

Rob had to fly to Florida the following week, on company business, and Lauren took advantage of his absence to go home for several days, over the next weekend. She hadn't seen her parents for a while because Rob liked her to be around at weekends so that they could see a lot of each other.

Her mother and father were delighted to have her home, and it was a peaceful, restful visit; only her sixteen-year-old sister, Lee, was at home at the same time. Lee was still at school, a skinny, ungainly teenager, with fairish brown hair and hazel eyes, sometimes moody, but with a wild sense of humour to compensate. Lauren was very fond of her; as they were the eldest and the youngest of the Bell children, there was a special rapport between them somehow. They went for walks together, swam in the local indoor pool, played tennis and one evening went to the cinema.

'I wish you came home more often,' Lee said as they walked home. 'It feels odd sometimes, being the only one left at home. It used to be such fun when all of us were together, but the house is very quiet these days.'

'Nat comes home quite often, doesn't she?'

'She used to, when she first went to university, but she hasn't been home for a few weeks.'

'A man?' Lauren raised an enquiring brow, and Lee giggled, nodding.

'She isn't talking about him, but I picked up his name—Edward. Imagine! How old-fashioned can you get? Not Eddy or Ned, just Edward, and he hates it if you shorten it, she said. But she says he's six feet and a college athlete, so he can't be as dull as he sounds.'

Lauren laughed. 'Natalie always goes for muscle men.'

'Yes, she does, doesn't she?' Lee said, struck by that thought. She slid an arm through Lauren's and nudged her affectionately. 'I wish you lived at home; I miss you.'

Lauren smiled at her. 'I miss you too, even if you do haunt the bathroom day and night, and steal my favourite perfume!'

'I do not!' Lee shrieked, but grinned, and they ran the rest of the way home.

Lauren was going home next day, but when she woke up the following morning she had all the symptoms of flu: a headache, a high temperature, a sore throat, the shivers. Her mother called the doctor, who shook his head over her.

'Probably caught it at the swimming pool—there's an epidemic at the moment; I've seen half a dozen cases so far today,' he said. 'Stay in bed, plenty of fluids, only a little light food—a boiled egg, poached fish, that sort of thing.' He wrote a prescription, handed it to her mother. 'See she takes this!' He glanced at his watch, restlessly on his way to the door almost before he had finished speaking.

'Thank you, Doctor,' Mrs Bell said, hurrying after him.

Lauren lay back against her pillows, swallowing with difficulty. What a nuisance! Any day now Rob would be back from the States. She would have to ring the office and explain, and they were not going to be pleased.

She lifted the phone and made the call; Annie was irritated. 'Flu? Are you sure it isn't just a cold? You've just had a couple of days off as well.'

'Come and visit me, to check up, if you don't believe me,' Lauren said in a hoarse, raw voice, and Annie sighed heavily.

'OK, OK. Sorry, but you aren't the first to call in sick, and I can see I'm going to have a problem getting the work done. Well, come back as soon as you can.' Annie hung up with a crash, and so did Lauren, glaring at the phone. How typical of Annie to refuse to believe in someone else's illness. Did she think Lauren would lie about it?

She certainly didn't want to be stuck here, in bed, feeling rotten. It was no fun, for one thing, being ill; and for another she longed to be in London to meet Rob at the airport when he arrived back. She missed him when he was away, and he had been away for almost two weeks now. It seemed far longer.

She sipped some lemon barley water, which relieved her throat a little, then lay back, her face wry. Absence certainly made the heart grow fonder. It put everything into perspective. Missing Rob made her remember why she had fallen in love with him in the first place. She shut her eyes and thought about him, smiling.

She hoped to be out of bed within a couple of days, but in fact she had the flu badly, and it was the end of the week before she was allowed up, and even then the doctor insisted that she must take another few days off work to recover.

'And you're not fit to make the journey back to London,' her mother said firmly. 'Stay here over the weekend, and then we'll see how you are on Monday, but no way are you going to drive your car while you're still so weak.'

'It's only flu, Mum!' protested Lauren. 'I'm not recovering from pneumonia!'

'And we don't want it to turn into pneumonia, do we?' said her mother, putting a rug round her legs and handing her a book. 'Stay there and read for an hour.'

As soon as she was alone, Lauren put down the book and stared into the sunny garden. Spring was in full bloom. A little clump of apple trees were pink and white with blossom, there were bright scarlet tulips lined along the paths dissecting the smoothly mowed lawns, the air was warm and sweet, and the birds were singing. It was a lovely day, and this was a wonderful view, but Lauren would rather have been in London with Rob.

He still hadn't returned from the States, though. She had left a message with his office, when she first fell ill, and he had rung her here a couple of times since then, and had sent her an enormous bouquet of flowers and a get well card. But he was very busy, and not a good letter writer, so it had been some days since she heard from him. She had no idea when he was coming back.

Frowning, she leaned over to pick up the phone. She didn't know where Rob was staying in the States; he hadn't expected to be there long, and hadn't given her a number. That was normal with them. He always called her, never the other way around. But she could call his office and ask when he would be back.

She got his newspaper, and asked for his extension. There was only a brief pause, then, 'Yes?' a curt voice asked.

She knew his secretary's voice, but it wasn't a girl who answered, it was a man, whose voice she also recognised, her face startled.

What was Sam Hardy doing in Rob's office? 'I wanted Mr Cornwell's secretary,' she said in a neutral tone, hoping he wouldn't recognise her voice.

There was a silence, then Sam said drily, 'She's off sick with the flu too, Lauren. How are you?'

She bit her lip, frowning. 'Better, thanks. I should be back soon. Is Rob back from the States yet?'

'No, but he might be back on Monday, I gather.'

Lauren smiled, delighted to hear that. 'Oh, that's great!' she said, her voice lifting with her mood. 'If I can persuade my parents I'm up to travelling I may be back then myself.'

'Taking the train back?' Sam sounded abstracted and indifferent, and Lauren answered as tersely.

'No, car.'

'After a bad dose of flu it would be stupid to try to drive all this way!' Sam told her, and his domineering voice made her teeth meet, made her scowl at the phone as if it were Sam himself.

She felt like snapping back at him, but instead she said coldly, 'If Rob rings, tell him I'll be back on Monday or Tuesday. Goodbye.'

She put the phone down and lay back, her face flushed and irritated. Every time she ran up against Sam he got under her skin in one way or another. It disturbed her that while she disliked him so intensely she should still feel a terrifying drag of attraction every time they met. Even talking to him on the phone was like touching a stinging nettle; one brush against it and her whole body reacted violently.

She ran a hand over her hot face, frowning. Stop thinking about him! she ordered herself, then picked up the book her mother had given her, a historical novel set during the reign of Richard the Third, and forced herself to concentrate on that.

When Lee had done her homework that evening they played cards for a couple of hours, giggling together, and then their mother despatched Lauren back to bed early with a cup of hot cocoa.

She spent the weekend in a leisurely fashion, sitting on the veranda of their house, or strolling around the garden with her family.

On the Sunday afternoon she looked so much better that her mother agreed that she could go back to London next day. 'But take the train, darling. I really don't think you should drive too far, and you can always pick your car up next weekend. You don't use it much in London anyway, do you?'

'Not during the week,' agreed Lauren sleepily. They were lying side by side on striped loungers on the lawn, and the sun was really quite hot for early May. Lauren wanted to get a tan, so she had put on a low-necked blue top which was cut off just above the midriff, and matching brief blue shorts which left most of her long legs bare.

'I think I'll go in and get some iced lemonade,' her mother said, getting up, with a yawn. 'Want some, darling?'

'Please,' said Lauren, without opening her eyes, and heard her mother walk away.

The sun poured down on her, the garden was full of sleepy sounds; a bee humming among the apple blossom, someone mowing their lawn, a butterfly flitting past, a fountain splashing in someone else's garden. It could almost be high summer, she thought. This had been a glorious weekend, and she was glad she hadn't spent it in London.

Her mother was taking a long time. Maybe one of her sisters had rung up? They often did on a Sunday afternoon, having some free time and knowing that someone was bound to be at home. The Bells were a closely knit family who never lost touch with each other for long.

She drifted into a doze until she heard the sound of movements, footsteps. Her mother was finally back with the lemonade.

'Mmm, at last!' she said, smiling without opening her eyes, stretched her arms above her head and yawned. 'I thought you'd never come!'

'I'd have come sooner if I'd realised you were waiting for me,' a voice drawled, and Lauren's eyes flew open in shock. It couldn't be! What on earth was he doing at her home?

Sam Hardy stood in front of her lounger, staring down at her, his cool eyes wandering slowly over her half-naked body. Lauren hadn't even been conscious that she was wearing so little until then, but now her skin heated and prickled with awareness.

She swung her bare legs off the lounger and stood up, grabbing a thin cotton wrap-around from the back of a chair; winding it hurriedly, with hands that trembled, around her body, tying the two ends just above her breasts.

'What are you doing here?' she muttered, angry because she was so intensely conscious of him.

Sam had been to her home once or twice while they were dating, but she still found it disturbing to see him here again, in this safe, familiar setting. It felt like an invasion, a threat, and her green eyes were nervous, flicking to his face and away again.

'You look like a boiled lobster; you shouldn't have been out here in this hot sun!' he murmured, taking a step closer and touching her arm with cool fingers.

She jumped instinctively, as though stung by a bee, and just as instinctively knocked his hand away. 'Don't!'

'What's wrong, Lauren?' he asked with ice-tipped mockery, smiling in an angry way. 'Does it bother you that much if I touch you?'

She knew her face was burning, and she wanted to hit him. 'I just don't like it!' she threw back at him, turning away to walk towards the house. She couldn't bear to stand there while he kept on looking at her with those speculative, tormenting eyes. She felt he could see right through the cotton wrap to what she had hidden under it; the smooth swell of her breasts, her pale-skinned midriff and slim hips, her bare thighs and long, bare legs. Sam Hardy had a way of looking at a woman that was like being touched, as if his eyes told you just what he was thinking. She had to get away.

She had only taken a few steps when a new thought hit her and she drew in a sharp breath, stiffening to swing round and face him again.

'Rob...nothing has happened to Rob? Has it? Has something happened to him?' She had visions of a car crash, or, worse, a plane crashing, everyone on board being killed. Whenever Rob flew long distances she felt this panic.

'No,' Sam said tersely, and she stopped babbling, breathing again.

'Oh.' The relief was short-lived, and she frowned again. 'Then *why* are *you* here?'

Sam eyed her with cool eyes, shrugging. 'I had the day off and it was good weather for a drive in the country, so I thought I'd kill two birds with one stone.'

She was wary, suspicious. 'What are you talking about?'

'I thought that if I drove out here I could drive you back to London,' he said. 'And make sure you didn't do something stupid, like drive yourself back before you were a hundred per cent better.'

Lauren caught her lower lip between her teeth, taken aback. 'Oh. I see. That was . . . that was a very kind thought, thank you.' Yes, it was kind, on the surface—but what ulterior motive might he have? Lauren didn't trust him.

He heard the uneasy reluctance in her tone, and his mouth indented with wry cynicism. 'I can't take all the credit,' he admitted. 'It was actually Annie's idea. After you rang the other day, I got on to her to tell her you'd be back soon. I said I thought you shouldn't make that journey alone, either in your car, or on the train, and Annie said she agreed, you shouldn't, but she needed you badly. Apparently, the flu has swept through the staff at *Ultra* like the plague, people keeling over on all sides, and Annie's pretty desperate to get you back.'

'And she asked you to pick me up?' Lauren found that hard to believe, but on the other hand Annie was more than capable of talking him into it.

'She suggested I might enjoy a drive in the country,' Sam told her drily, and the deviousness of that did sound like Annie.

'Well, I'll go and pack,' she said, moving towards the house, and he walked with her, his shadow leaping ahead, black on the white walls.

Her mother met them, a polite uncertain smile ready. 'Where are you going, darling?' she asked Lauren.

'Upstairs to pack. Sam's going to drive me back to London.' Lauren gave her a teasing smile. 'You didn't want me to drive myself, so that should make you happy.'

It was obvious that it didn't. Mrs Bell didn't know exactly what had happened between these two, but she did know that her daughter had broken with Sam long ago and hadn't seen him since.

She was puzzled by his reappearance, and wondered uneasily what it meant. Mrs Bell had never been one to pry into her children's love lives, and Lauren had not, for years, confided her secret thoughts to her mother, but her parents were delighted by her engagement to Rob. They were very happy about the utter solidity of her future with the heir to the Cornwell millions. Oh, they had been taken aback at first, it had amazed them, the news of her engagement. They were not ambitious for their children in any material sense, but they loved her and wanted her to be safe and happy, and they thought she would be with Rob.

They certainly did not want anything to wreck her chances of marrying a man who could give her so much, and her mother's eyes uneasily assessed Sam Hardy as a man who could destroy, a dangerous man. She might be well over fifty, but Sarah Bell was still very much a female, and she recognised in Sam Hardy an intensely sexy man.

She fell back on her usual panacea for dealing with a difficult man. 'Can I get you a drink, Mr Hardy? Have you eaten?'

Soothe the savage breast, Lauren thought, hiding a smile, feed the tiger. Wickedly, she left her mother to talk to him, wishing she could be an invisible witness to their conversation. Her mother was going to probe away delicately, trying not to let him see what she was doing—and Sam was going to be only too well aware what was going on, and would no doubt be highly amused.

She took off her shorts and top and showered rapidly before changing into white jeans and a blue sweatshirt, then began to pack. Lee came in from a visit to a school friend and paused in the doorway to watch her. 'What's Sam Hardy doing here? I thought you'd dumped him.'

'Who told you about him? You're too young to remember him!' Lauren frowned, closing her case and clicking the locks.

'I had a terrific crush on him for months,' said Lee with a dreamy smile.

'Oh, did you indeed?' Lauren looked at her with a mixture of amusement and irritation. Sam Hardy had the same effect on every woman he met, however young or old, and it annoyed the hell out of Lauren. 'Well, now you're old enough to have more sense! Sam Hardy should have a government health warning stamped on his forehead.'

Lee giggled. 'That's what makes him so sexy! The thrill of the danger, the lure of the forbidden...'

Lauren threw a pillow at her and Lee took a spectacular dive sideways, landing on the bed where she lay full length, her chin propped on her hands. 'Seriously, Loll...'

'Don't call me that!'

'Oh, Lauren, then... seriously, what's Sam Hardy doing here?'

'My editor sent him to get me,' Lauren explained.

'I wish she'd send him to get me!' Lee sighed. She had a skinny, moody face, but with a flush of excitement on her skin and her eyes brilliant with interest she was quite striking, and Lauren looked at her with protective affection. She hated the thought of her youngest sister getting hurt, but Lee was so sensitive, so vulnerable, that Lauren was afraid for her. How would Lee cope with the pitfalls of adult love?

'Carry my case down for me?' asked Lauren gently, and Lee sprang up in that sudden way of hers and grabbed the case, heading for the door with it. Lauren lingered to take a last look around her old room, almost reluctant to leave it although she had been eager to get back to London only a few hours ago.

When she got downstairs, she found Lee chattering away to Sam in the hall. 'It must be so thrilling to photograph history as it's happening! I'd love to do your job.'

'It can be dangerous, don't forget!' Sam said, and Lee bristled.

'For a girl, you mean?' Her feminism was newminted and aggressive. Sam considered her flushed face with wry eyes.

'For either sex. I was scared stiff most of the time while I was in a war zone—only a lunatic wouldn't be. When you might get a bullet in the back at any moment you stop thinking of camera angles and getting a good picture and start praying you'll survive.'

Lee laughed. 'I bet! Do you think you'll ever go back to the job, or are you going to stay in London now?'

Sam shrugged. 'London, probably.' He gave a sideways, glinting smile, full of flirtation. 'I'm getting old.'

Lee hooted, delighted to have Sam flirt with her. 'You're just fishing for compliments! Well, I'm not rising to it!'

Lauren watched her sister sparkling up at Sam while he smiled at her with such indulgent enjoyment, and her teeth met. Did he have to flirt with every female he met, even if they were still at school?

Sam turned, his eyes narrowing at her expression, and his smile vanishing. 'Ready?'

'Yes,' Lauren said through her teeth.

Sam swept an all-seeing look from her smoothly brushed blonde head down over her casual jeans and top to the trainers she wore on her feet. His crooked eyebrow was disparaging, and her angry flush darkened, but he said nothing, just picked up her case to carry it out to his car while she was saying goodbye to her parents and Lee.

'Do look after yourself,' her mother said anxiously, and Lauren sensed that she was not merely talking about her health. Sarah Bell was worried about the reappearance of Sam Hardy, and his possible effect on Lauren. 'You shouldn't go back to work right away. That was bad flu you had.'

'I know—I'll be careful,' she promised, on the surface meaning that she would look after her health, while her eyes assured her mother that she wasn't a fool; she wouldn't allow Sam Hardy within ten feet of her.

Of course, she knew that whatever she said to her mother Annie would get her own way. If half the office was off with the flu, what else could she do but go back to work and help Annie get the magazine out?

Sam Hardy, though, was a different matter. She meant every word about him. It wasn't merely that she did not trust him—she did not trust herself where he was concerned either. He had a disturbing effect on her metabolism. Every time he was around she found herself watching him, reacting to him. It was purely a chemical reaction—she put all the blame on her damned hormones. It really didn't mean anything, it couldn't, because she loved Rob and she certainly did not love Sam Hardy, but Lauren was worried by it, all the same, and she meant to take every precaution to keep Sam at arm's length.

It was dusk by the time they set off. Sam looked at his watch and thought aloud. 'We should be in London by nine, if we're lucky with the traffic. We could stop en route to have a snack, if you're hungry?'

'No, thanks,' she said tersely. She didn't want to spend any more time in his company than she had to.

He gave her a sideways glance, his mouth hard. 'Just as you like.' He drove on in silence and Lauren settled back, her eyes on the road ahead, trying to pretend she wasn't aware of him sitting there beside her. She wasn't letting her eyes stray to him, yet she was deeply, reluctantly conscious of him all the time; the cool control of his long-fingered hands on the steering wheel, the slim, muscled legs stretched out beside her own, the hard profile, that stubborn male jawline, and most of all the mouth above it.

She frowned, wishing he had never come back to work in London, wishing he had stayed abroad. But then he might have been killed, she thought, flinching from the thought. She didn't want that. The idea of Sam dying... a shiver ran down her spine. Her mind was in such a tangle; she didn't know what she felt, or thought, any more. She closed her eyes and tried to sleep, or at least make Sam think she was sleeping. It was the only protective device she could come up with.

He apparently fell for it, because he didn't speak again until they reached London and parked outside her flat; then he got out, took her case out of the car and insisted on carrying it to her flat, in spite of Lauren's protests.

'You're pale and you look tired,' he said flatly. 'Look at the way you slept for most of the drive!'

She couldn't answer that without admitting she had been pretending, so she hurried to unlock her front

door, then turned to take the case, but Sam shot
smoothly past her into the flat and put the case down
to her little sitting-room, glancing around curiously.

'You've changed the wallpaper.' It had been a
creamy pink with tiny flowers on it; now it was cool
green, with leaves twining everywhere, and gave the
room a deliciously underwater look. 'Did you do it
yourself?' asked Sam, and she nodded.

'Too expensive to pay someone else.' She wondered
how to get rid of him, without a scene. He looked as
if he was in no hurry to leave, and it disturbed her to
have him here, in her flat, alone with her. The intimacy was undermining.

Sam explored lazily, picking up ornaments, studying pictures on the walls, looking at the books in her
little bookcase. 'You still read too many novels,' he
said, with a sidelong smile that for some reason made
her stomach plunge. If he was going to start flirting
with her she would scream.

'That's right,' she said with a touch of defiance.
'Thanks very much for the lift, it was very good of
you. You must be dying to get home yourself—it must
have been tiring, driving to my home and straight back
again.' She stood at the door in an obvious way, and
Sam turned, his mouth leashed, and walked towards
her.

Lauren stiffened as he drew level with her, her back
against the wall, her head up, her mouth dry. Every
nerve in her body seemed to be twanging like a taut

guitar string as he paused, staring down into her eyes
with a hypnotic intensity.

'One day you and I are going to have to have a
showdown,' he bit out, his brows threatening, then he
walked past, and she sagged against the wall in relief
as she heard the front door slam.

CHAPTER FIVE

LAUREN went back to work next morning, and Annie welcomed her with open arms. 'I was beginning to think I'd have to get the magazine out all by myself! Two more people called in sick so far this morning!' She gestured to the chair on the other side of her desk. 'Sit, and we'll sort out your jobs for today.' Annie's desk was normally clear and tidy, but today it looked as if a blizzard of paper had hit it. And Annie rummaged through it all, sending up showers of clippings, copy sheets, old magazines, like a dog digging up a rabbit hole.

'Here we are!' she said, emerging with a list in her hand. 'Now, this is what I want you to do...' She paused to stare at Lauren fixedly. 'You are quite better, I hope? You look rather pale.'

'I'm fine,' Lauren reassured her, unable to admit that she had had a sleepless night. That was not, after all, anything to do with her illness—it was all Sam Hardy's fault, but Lauren couldn't tell Annie why she was pale and had dark circles under her green eyes.

'Well, I hope you are, because I'll have to give you a pretty heavy work load,' Annie said wryly, and from then on Lauren at least had no time to fret over the problem of Sam Hardy; she was much too busy.

Rob got back two days later, and rang Lauren in the office, sounding weary and half asleep. 'Jet lag,' he moaned. 'God, how I hate transatlantic flights! I should have come back on Concorde, but I got a lift in a private jet.'

'Poor darling,' sympathised Lauren, feeling pretty exhausted herself although several other reporters had come back to work and things were gradually getting back to normal. All the same, while she talked to Rob she was automatically subbing a piece of copy in front of her. 'Did your trip go well, otherwise?'

'Yes, thanks,' he said, yawning. 'Oh, I can hardly keep my eyes open—sorry, Lauren. I think I'd better go home to bed! I've been so hectically busy for weeks that that flight was the last straw. I'll ring you when I'm back to normal, OK? At the moment I'm in no state to talk.'

She put the phone down feeling flat and puzzled. There had been something odd in Rob's voice; he had sounded . . . distant, touchy. Almost as though he was angry—with her? But why?

The reporters' room was empty—everyone else was out on a story, and she was alone. She stood up and walked to the window, looked out, frowning. They hadn't seen each other for some weeks; she couldn't imagine why Rob should be angry with her.

A little flush crept up her face. Unless he had heard about Sam driving down to her home to pick her up? Had Sam Hardy mentioned it to him? She remembered Rob's spiky reaction when she admitted having once been involved with Sam—was he jealous?

Or was she just feeling guilty because when Sam drove her back to London the atmosphere between them had been tense? Her flush deepened and she shifted restlessly. Nothing had happened, though! OK, she had felt a silent pull of attraction, a nagging awareness of him, but she hadn't let it show; Sam couldn't have known what was going on inside her.

Oh, don't be so ridiculous! a little voice inside her head said. Sam's no fool, he felt it too. It was there between us all the time, like leaking electricity, making flashes and sparks in the air.

But he wouldn't go and boast to Rob about it, or to anyone else! Sam was a lot of things, but he wasn't the type to talk about his women.

I am not one of his women! she told herself furiously. I'd rather die than be one too.

She turned away and walked back to her desk, her face set and grim, and forced herself to concentrate on her work.

Maybe she had imagined that distant note in Rob's voice, anyway. Poor love, he was tired, that was all. He must be exhausted by his American trip—it had meant a lot to him to succeed over there, and impress his father. Rob had an inferiority complex where Charles Cornwell was concerned; he was always trying to show his father he was a chip off the old block, but so far he hadn't really managed it. Maybe this time he finally had?

On her way to lunch next day she saw a job being advertised on the internal notice board and read the typed words with excitement. It was the sort of opening she always looked for; a reporter's job on the *Gazette*. It only had one drawback—Sam Hardy worked there too. But so did Rob, which was a big plus, so Lauren went back to her desk there and then and spent her lunch hour applying for the job.

She rang Rob several times that day, but he was always out. 'Mr Cornwell is very busy,' his secretary informed her coolly. 'I'll tell him you called.'

Lauren suspected she did nothing of the kind, because Rob didn't ring her back until the evening, and then was in a rush to go to a reception at one of the embassies, with his father and a party of important visitors from overseas.

'I'm sorry, Lauren, I've got to go tonight, Dad insists, so I can't get out of it. I'm up to my eyes in work at the moment, unfortunately.'

Lauren bit her lip. 'Rob, is something wrong?'

'Wrong?' He sounded abstracted, very far away. 'What do you mean, wrong? I'm just horribly busy these days; Dad's piling on the work and won't take any excuses.' His voice changed, took on an excited note. 'Oh, I forgot to tell you, he's going to put me on the board at the end of the year—he says I've earned it and it's time I was there to support him. I really think Dad is starting to take me seriously at last!'

'That's wonderful,' Lauren said, smiling. Maybe she had been overreacting, reading the situation quite the wrong way round? Maybe Rob was genuinely busy, trying to please and impress his father—and his feelings for her hadn't changed at all?

'I'm so glad, Rob,' she added. 'But when am I going to see you? It's ages since we saw each other.'

'Yes,' Rob said slowly. 'Of course... There's a lot to tell you, it's just that I'm so busy... Hang on, let me look in my diary and see what I can manage this week. Look, Lauren, how about dinner on Friday?'

'Friday, lovely. I'll look forward to hearing all about your trip,' Lauren said. 'See you in the wine-bar after work for a drink first?'

Rob hesitated, then said, 'Yes, in the wine bar—six-thirty. Lauren...' He paused, clearing his throat. 'Lauren, I'm sorry about all this, but Dad... Well, it isn't fair to blame Dad, it's just the way things have fallen out, but I'm sorry I'm letting you down...'

'Don't worry about it, darling,' she said warmly, smiling at the huskiness of his voice. Poor Rob, he was being torn two ways, she saw that now. 'I understand, and I'm not angry with you,' she said, and Rob gave a long sigh.

'Do you? Thanks, Lauren, you're an angel.' His voice changed again, became crisper. 'I must go, someone just called me... see you on Friday, and I'll tell you everything then.'

On that Friday morning she got a letter from the personnel manager at the *Gazette* telling her that she had been short-listed for the job she had applied for—and for the rest of the day she was walking on air.

She had time after work on Friday evening, before going across the road to meet Rob at the wine-bar, to change out of the pleated grey skirt and crisp blue and white striped blouse she had worn all day into a much more glamorous outfit.

The little black dress she chose to wear wasn't new, she had had it for years, but it always looked good on her, and made her feel good, because it came from an excellent designer and was both elegant and beautifully styled. Rob had always admired it.

She had pearl studs in her ears, one thin string of good artificial pearls around her neck, which she had been given by her grandfather on her eighteenth birthday. Her blonde hair gleamed brightly against the black jersey silk; her carefully applied eye-shadow gave her green eyes a glittering setting, and she had painted her mouth a warm coral pink.

She wanted to look her best for Rob tonight; they had been apart for weeks, and she sensed a change in their relationship and wasn't sure if it had begun in her or in Rob. She couldn't deny that she had been feeling restless, uncertain, for a long time, and perhaps he had sensed that? Or was Rob unsettled because his father was permanently trying to undermine the way Rob felt about her? It must be tough on him, having to fight his father over her all the time.

She arrived punctually, but there was no sign of Rob at any of the tables in the wine-bar, so she sat down at an empty table and ordered a glass of white wine. Several people, colleagues from work, nodded and smiled at her, and someone walking past her table stopped and asked, 'Meeting someone?'

'Rob,' she smiled.

'Rob Cornwell?' the other girl said, looking at her in a funny way. 'Oh, well, have a good time.'

She walked away, and Lauren looked wryly at her retreating back—Jean Hood had a streak of spite in her nature, she had always been jealous whenever she saw Lauren with Rob; maybe she had always fancied him too?

Lauren sipped her wine and looked out of the window, watching the road to catch sight of Rob running across from the office block opposite. The minutes ticked past. She looked at her watch, frowning. Rob was a quarter of an hour late. He had said he was very busy; maybe he had been held up?

She had finished her wine, and decided not to order another until Rob got there, so she nibbled a few roast almonds from the bowl of mixed nuts on the table. Another surreptitious glance at her watch told her Rob was now twenty minutes late. Should she order another glass of wine? Ring his office to see how much longer he would be?

There was some giggling from Jean Hood's table. Lauren turned round and found Jean and her friends watching her. They all looked away, whispering, their voices too low for her to catch, but she sensed they were talking about her—perhaps they thought Rob had stood her up?

She fidgeted with her empty glass, her head lowered and a flush on her face. Then the door opened and she looked eagerly towards it, her teeth meeting and her body tensing as she saw that it wasn't Rob who had come in—it was Sam Hardy.

It would be, she thought bitterly. That was all she needed. Not only had Rob not kept their date, Sam Hardy was here to witness her being stood up. Why did he have to arrive just now?

He stood by the door, looking around the wine-bar. Lauren pretended not to have seen him.

She kept her eyes fixed on the pavement outside, her head turned away, but as if she had antennae she knew when he began to walk towards her.

He slipped into the seat opposite her. 'Hello, Lauren.' His voice was dry; he knew she was trying to ignore him.

She looked across the table, deliberately making her face cool and offhand. 'Hello. I'm waiting for someone, so would you mind taking another table?'

'I have to talk to you,' he said quietly, his grey eyes fixed on her face. 'Alone, in private, Lauren.'

'I don't want to talk to you in private!' she snapped, irritated by his obstinacy. 'Look, my date will be here any minute——'

'No,' Sam said, and her eyes focused on his face then, her own expression stilled, apprehensive. Sam stared back at her and added grimly, 'Come outside, Lauren. I think you'll want to hear this news where nobody can see your face.'

She went white. 'It's Rob,' she whispered, and he nodded. Her imagination leapt with terrible images— Rob in a car crash, Rob badly injured, Rob dying. 'What's happened?' she got out hoarsely.

Sam got up and reached down for her hand, jerked her to her feet and guided her out of the wine-bar.

Vaguely, Lauren was aware of watching eyes, of whispering, but she wasn't thinking about Jean Hood or any of the others from the firm. She was barely able to move one foot in front of another. Her fear and anxiety almost paralysed her.

'What's happened?' she asked Sam, husky with anxiety. 'Tell me, for God's sake!'

'Wait just a minute.' Sam had his car a few yards down the road; he unlocked it and slid her into the passenger seat, got behind the wheel, started the engine.

'What are you doing?' Lauren demanded, stiffening, grabbing his arm. 'Turn off the ignition— I'm not going anywhere with you. Tell me what's happened to Rob— I have to know…is he hurt? Is he…' She broke off, swallowing, refusing to put her worst fears into words. 'We had a date tonight, I was waiting for him. I was just getting anxious…'

'He won't be meeting you tonight,' Sam said curtly. 'Or any other night.'

She caught her breath, shock keeping her very still. Rob had to be dead—there was a grim finality about the way Sam spoke, the tense way he was watching her, his brows heavy.

Then he said, 'He's at his engagement party,' and her green eyes flashed wide open, stunned.

'What?'

'He's going to marry Janice Earl.'

Lauren was bewildered, she shook her head stupidly. 'He's engaged to *me*.' She looked down at the hands shaking in her lap, at Rob's ring glittering on her finger, as if for confirmation, for visible proof. Sam had confused and disturbed her. 'We talked on the phone, he would have said…something… He was taking me out to dinner tonight…' Her head came up and she stared at him in accusation, cried out angrily, 'Why are you lying to me? You don't think I'm going to believe this! It's ridiculous.' She thought of the flame-haired, feline girl Sam had brought to that party and muttered, 'He hardly knows Janice Earl; they only met once, at that party you brought her to!'

'They saw a lot of each other while he was over in the States recently. Charlie Cornwell's doing a big deal with Janice's father—that was what kept Rob over there so long.'

Lauren drew a sharp breath. 'Is his father behind this? Was it him who sent you to talk to me? He's been trying to break us up for months—he hates me. He probably made this story up, about her and Rob…wishful thinking…he hopes I'll quarrel with Rob over it, but——'

'Don't be a fool, Lauren!' Sam bit out in a thick angry voice. 'Charlie may be over the moon about Janice and his son, but it wasn't him who sent me to talk to you, and I'm telling you the truth, don't kid yourself otherwise.'

She felt as if her stomach had dropped out of her. Her skin was icy cold and she was shaking. She sensed he was telling the truth, but she couldn't bear to believe it. 'Rob didn't like her,' she protested wildly. 'He said she was a spoilt little bitch!'

'Janice has more decent instincts than he does, anyway,' Sam said acidly. 'He was going to leave you sitting there; he didn't care how you'd feel about that, not knowing what had happened. The guy's a creep; a selfish, cowardly creep. He chickened out of telling you in person. He was going to tell you tonight, I gather; that was the idea of meeting you—but his father decided tonight was the perfect occasion for announcing their engagement.'

'Rob would have rung me to break our date then!'

'He couldn't face you in the end. Instead he wrote you a letter, then forgot to post it. Janice spotted it on his desk when she went to his office to pick him up...'

Lauren's whole body flinched in pain at the thought of the other girl collecting Rob from his office, seeing the letter addressed to her, and knowing what it must contain. How could Rob do this to her?

Sam's level voice went on beside her, 'He confessed that he'd been going to see you tonight, to explain and break off with you. She thought he already had—he'd promised he would when he first came back from the States, and when she asked he'd said he'd told you. He's a liar as well as a cheat, your wonderful Rob. As they drove past the wine-bar a quarter of an hour ago, Janice saw you in there, waiting...'

Hot, humiliated blood rushed up Lauren's face. She bit down hard on her lip, to stifle a cry of pain.

Sam stared straight ahead, talking flatly. 'She was horrified. She rang me on the car phone and asked me to go to the wine-bar and tell you.'

Lauren swallowed on sickness, closed her eyes and leaned her head on the car window, unable to speak.

Sam suddenly started the car and drove off fast, and she was grateful for the silence between them, for she was afraid she might start to cry any minute. Why had it been him? Fate had a strange sense of humour. Fate and Janice Earl, she thought bitterly. Why on earth had she picked on Sam? Because he was the only person she knew who also knew Lauren? Well, she had picked the worst possible messenger of doom. Sam Hardy was the last person Lauren would have wanted around at this particular moment.

The car stopped. Opening her eyes reluctantly, Lauren looked out and saw that he had driven her home; they were parked outside her flat.

She couldn't meet Sam's eyes, so she just said flatly, 'Thanks for the lift home,' and got out of the car. Her legs felt weak under her, and it didn't help to hear Sam get out of the car behind her. His door slammed and his long legs swiftly covered the ground between them. He caught her up as she got to the entrance of the flats.

'Go away,' she muttered. 'Please!'

'I just want to see you safely inside your flat,' he said with grim determination, and she was too miserable to argue with him. When they reached her front door, she got out her key and tried to fit it into the lock, but dropped it and then couldn't see it on the floor. Her eyes were blurred, as if she was in a mist. Sam silently picked up the key; she heard the door unlock, open.

'Thanks, goodnight,' she said thickly without looking at him, and stumbled inside. She pushed the door shut, then realised Sam was on the same side of it. She didn't look at his face, just saw his long legs, beside her, in silky black trousers; he was wearing an evening suit, she realised for the first time. She hadn't really seen him before, there had been too much on her mind. He must have been on his way to a party when Janice rang. Maybe it had been her party, to celebrate her engagement to Rob?

Lauren started to laugh at the irony of that, and the laughter became crying—the tears which had been blinding her for some time now poured down her face, and she shook and sobbed, leaning on the wall, her face hidden from the man beside her.

Sam let her cry for a couple of minutes, then he put his arms about her. She resisted, trying to stop crying, but he firmly pulled her round so that she was leaning on him. Lauren couldn't get away, but she didn't want him to see her face, so she buried it in his jacket. She could smell his aftershave; a fresh, pine scent that made her think of her home, of the woods beyond the garden there, of high fir trees swaying in a crisp spring wind and the cry of the birds.

Homesickness overwhelmed her. She wished she was there, she longed to go home. On Monday everyone in the firm would know, everyone would stare, whisper—it would be number one item on the gossip scene, her broken engagement, the news that Rob was planning to marry Janice Earl.

'Come on, Lauren,' Sam said quietly. 'This isn't the end of the world, you know. You'll get over him. Just keep telling yourself what a creep he is, and that you're well rid of him.'

She ran a shaky hand over her wet eyes before lifting her head, and was surprised by his expression. His voice sounded cool enough, but his face was tight and blank, his eyes sombre under their dark brows. For the first time she wondered how he had felt about Janice Earl. Sam's affairs had never lasted long or seemed to have any depth, she had never heard of him being hit by the ending of a relationship, but he seemed to be taking this very personally. He looked as angry as she felt, and she couldn't believe he felt this badly because of sympathy for her!

'Look, I am grateful, you've been very kind,' she said slowly, watching him. 'But I want to be alone now, could you go, please?'

'Are you sure you're all right?' Sam didn't move, nor did he release her, and she gave him a derisive, cynical little smile.

'What do you think I might do? Kill myself.'

Sam stiffened, his frown carving deep lines into his temples.

She laughed angrily at him. 'Oh, don't look like that! Rob made a fool of me, but I've got more self-respect than to do anything that stupid! I shan't be killing myself over Rob Cornwell. I won't even kill him, although at the moment I'd like to! What I might do is ring a rival paper and give them a beauty of a story about what Rob just did to me! They'd jump at it wouldn't they? Newspaper proprietor's son dumps working girl fiancée to marry millionaire's daughter! Pure Fleet Street. They'd pay me a fortune for it.'

'You wouldn't do it, though,' Sam said quietly, and she pushed him away irritably. He let his arms drop to his sides, leaving her free.

'Why shouldn't I?' she muttered, very flushed. 'He deserves it! They all do, Rob and his father, and that girl. They've been utterly ruthless with me—why shouldn't I be ruthless with them?'

'Two reasons,' said Sam in that careful, level voice. 'First, it would be as despicable as Rob has been, and you aren't like him. Why sink to his level? You're too honest to sell your own story—you know what the gutter Press would make of it!'

'I know how Charlie Cornwell and his precious son would feel reading about themselves in the gutter press! They'd hate it.'

'I'm sure they would,' Sam agreed drily. 'But there's the other reason why you shouldn't sell the story— you'd lose your job. Charlie Cornwell wouldn't hesitate. In fact, you'd be doing him a favour—he'd love an excuse to fire you.'

Her mouth twisted as she thought about that. 'Yes, you're right—he would too, the bastard. What sort of world is this? He and his son have treated me badly, but if I tell anyone he'll take my job away.' She breathed fiercely, her hands clenched. 'It isn't fair!'

'No,' agreed Sam drily. 'But then this isn't a fair world. You're an adult, Lauren; you must have discovered that a long time ago.' His mouth went crooked, his grey eyes glittered. 'Pain is a part of being alive, I'm afraid. The only way never to get hurt is never to live at all, and especially never to fall in love.'

'Well, on that subject you must be the expert! I don't suppose you've ever been in love in your life!' she muttered, and heard him take a sharp breath.

'Thanks!' His voice was harsh, and she bit her lip, her lashes down, but watching him through them, frowning. His face was drawn and shadowed—had he really been in love with Janice?

'Well, have you?' she asked, distracted from her own feelings for a moment by an intense curiosity about his. Wouldn't it be ironic if the first time Sam Hardy actually fell in love the woman walked out on him, the way he had on so many other women?

Sam's mouth twisted in anger. 'Why do you want to know? Would it make you feel better to know I'd been through it too? OK, if it will help—why not? Yes, Lauren, I have been in love, and there was no happy ending for me either. Maybe there's no such thing. I stopped believing in fairy-tales a long time ago. After all, I'm thirty-five years old.' He looked her over, his black brows arched, his smile suddenly mocking. 'And you're no adolescent either.'

'In four years I'll be thirty,' she said bleakly. 'Do you think I'm not very aware of that?'

'Thirty is a watershed,' Sam agreed, and she had a sudden sense of *déjà vu*.

She had heard him say that before, surely? The memory came to her in a flash just a second later. Sam had said it once before, in her hearing; at a party he gave on his thirty-first birthday, in his flat, which had been packed with people. She had hardly known him then. They had only just met for the first time; she was still serving an apprenticeship and studying journalism at a college two days a week, while she worked the rest of the time. She was only twenty-two, and she had been dazzled by him, light-headed with excitement. She had been falling in love with the speed of light. Of course, that was before she had met Annette, and heard about Sam's past track record.

'You've got a long way to go, and a lot to learn,' Sam drawled, looking wry.

How strange that the icy hostility between them seemed to have gone now, because they had both been jilted by someone else. There was a pattern there, but she was too tired to think about it.

She yawned abruptly, feeling so weary that she had to lean back against the wall to stay on her feet. 'Sam, I can't talk any more. I need to be alone. I'm not going to do anything stupid, just lie down and maybe get some sleep. You've been very kind, and I'm grateful, but please go...'

He ran a glance over her face, his grey eyes like searchlights hunting in the shadows, then nodded, his mouth indenting. 'Take the phone off the hook before you go to bed, and don't dream about Rob Cornwell.'

'How do I control my dreams?' she asked bitterly.

'I'd better give you something else to dream about,' Sam muttered, and the next second his mouth was on hers, and his arms were round her so tightly that she could barely breathe, let alone get away.

She struggled, pulling away, flushed and violently angry—what did he think he was doing? The last thing she wanted was to have a man touch her! Didn't he realise that?

She tried to tell him so, to shout at him to let her go, but she couldn't say anything—his mouth was too insistent, muffling her words.

He wouldn't let her turn her head away, or push him back. He moved one hand up to the back of her head and held it there; his lips parting hers in a compulsive demand that left her helpless. She had to give way to it, her head forced back, her throat stretched. She couldn't breathe, she was suffocating, she couldn't even think any more.

Sam's body seemed to be touching hers at every point; he was moving restlessly against her, an intimate contact that sent a strange tremor running through her. She felt very odd, as if she might be going to faint. Her eyelids were as heavy as lead, she couldn't keep them open. The hands pushing at his shoulders curled into his smooth evening jacket, clenching and unclenching on the material.

Maybe he was right? Why shouldn't she have something else to dream about? Anything to forget the pain and humiliation Rob had just inflicted on her...

Eyes shut, she began to kiss him back, her arms going round his neck, her hands running through his dark, warm hair. They had never been lovers during that brief affair, long ago. She hadn't been ready to sleep with him, something for which she had been grateful later. She could remember wanting him, though, a frustrated ache of desire deep inside her, and her body remembered those feelings now as she arched against him, a moan of response in her throat, a deep, soft purr of pleasure.

Sam's hands had loosed their powerful grip once she stopped fighting; they moved up and down her back, pushing her closer, they explored her body, touching her softly, a sensuous caress which made her sigh and cling closer, kissing him hungrily.

Sam groaned, his face against her throat, his voice husky, thickened by passion, as he muttered words that were barely coherent. '...wanted you so long, Lauren...waited for this for years...'

Alarm bells rang in her head and she stiffened, her eyes flying open. What? What was he saying? He sounded exultant, triumphant, and all Lauren's aroused excitement drained away.

She had been too busy thinking of herself; she hadn't thought about Sam or what he would be getting out of his kindness to her—but now she did, and her face whitened and turned ice-cold.

It was obvious, of course—how had she been so blind? Sam hadn't followed her into her flat because he was worried about her, or wanted to comfort her. His motives were nothing so noble. He hadn't been trying to distract her or put Rob out of her mind on the spur of the moment either. He had had something like this planned from the very beginning. She had been set up.

Oh, Janice had rung him, no doubt, and asked him to go over to the wine-bar to see her, and break the news to her, but Sam had seized a golden opportunity with both hands. He had realised she was in a state of shock at the news that Rob had jilted her, and he had taken cold-blooded advantage of the fact to make a play for her himself.

He must have been waiting for years to revenge himself on her for walking out on him before he had even got her into bed, and he had seen his chance to-night.

She had frozen on the spot, standing very still, like a pale statue, while she worked it all out—and Sam suddenly seemed to realise that something was wrong. He lifted his head, his face darkly flushed, his breathing rapid, and stared down at her with a faint frown, his grey eyes searching her face.

'Don't go cold on me, Lauren, not now, not this time,' he said huskily, and ran caressing fingertips down her cheek to her mouth, gently stroking her lips, staring at her with eyes that seemed to her to glitter with elation. 'I'm going crazy, I want you so much...'

'I'm sorry,' she said in a stiff little voice, forcing herself to stare back at him because she knew that if she looked away he wouldn't believe she meant it. 'I can't. I thought I could, but I can't. I tried to pretend you were Rob, but it doesn't work...'

She saw the shock of what she had said in his face. He tensed and paled, the excited flush, the brilliance of his eyes all going and a harshness tightening the lines of mouth and jaw.

'What are you talking about? You wanted me a moment ago! Do you think I don't know? You can't hide it—I know you wanted me as much as I wanted you...'

'All right, I did,' she said with a defiant look. 'For a while...but only because I was pretending you were Rob!'

Sam looked as if she had slapped him round the face. 'I don't believe you! You're lying...you wanted me, not him. You'd forgotten him...'

Lauren was on the verge of tears now. She was so tired. It had been a very bad evening and she wanted some peace; she wanted Sam to go away and stop bullying her. So she closed her eyes and let the tears escape from under her lids, let them run down her cheeks, their saltiness moist on her mouth, and sobbed.

'I can't forget Rob—how could I? I love him... Oh, leave me alone, go away, and leave me alone...'

Sam stood there for a moment longer, his fingers biting into her shoulders, then he almost threw her aside and went. She heard the front door slam, and she was alone at last.

She rubbed her wet face angrily and then she went to bed, not expecting to sleep, but needing the darkness and silence around her, as if she could hide in them and forget everything. In fact she did; she fell asleep almost at once, and slept heavily, although it was a troubled sleep, shot with dreams that made her toss about restlessly.

Faces mocked her; laughed at her. She kept seeing a man at a distance, vanishing around corners, and felt a frantic need to catch up with him, but kept losing him again. 'Rob, Rob,' she called after him, running faster, along corridors that turned into a green-hedged maze, turning round and round back on itself, confusing and disorientating her, and then at last she saw Rob just ahead of her and he turned to hold out his arms. She ran sobbing into them.

But it wasn't Rob. It was Sam Hardy, and his face was a glittering threat that made her cry out in fear, and then he kissed her, and the fear became an urgent desire which made her body burn.

She woke up with a moan of shame from that dream, at dawn, with first light, went into the kitchen and made herself some strong coffee, and lay in bed still trembling after what she had dreamt.

After a while she calmed down enough to begin thinking, rather than feeling. In the first stunning shock of being jilted she hadn't had time to disentangle her deeper emotions from the surface ones. At the back of her mind, she realised, she had never been quite sure of Rob. He was from such a different background; marrying him would have been like marrying Prince Charming, and Lauren had never quite believed such fairy-tales came true for ordinary girls like her, especially since his father was so angrily opposed to the idea.

It had hurt, though, to lose him, especially in such a way—to be jilted without warning, to know Rob had fallen for another woman. It had been a shock, and what happened later with Sam had made it all much worse.

She had been angry with him for so long now—it was her usual condition where Sam Hardy was concerned—but that morning she found she was past anger. She despised and hated him. Knowing that she was emotionally off balance, he had tried to seduce her—how low could you sink? What sort of man did something like that?

Sam Hardy, that was who! she thought, her green eyes fierce. He was ready to use any weapon, take any advantage, to get what he wanted—and he had never forgotten that she had been one woman who had got away before he got her into bed, so he had been waiting all this time for a chance to add her scalp to the others hanging from his belt!

Well, he could forget that. She'd make sure he never got another chance. In future she would avoid him like the plague.

CHAPTER SIX

ROB'S letter arrived later that morning. Lauren read it bleakly, hearing his voice through the words: Rob, being charming, placating, self-pitying.

He had written in a hurry, by hand; Rob's handwriting was large, confident, with a tendency to become a scrawl, and she had to guess at some of the words. He told her he had to break their engagement; he was sorry, he felt badly, he knew how she must feel—but with every sentence it became only too clear that Rob was more concerned with his own feelings than with hers. He was trying to wriggle out of their engagement without collecting any blame.

He justified himself with special pleading; said he hadn't been able to stop himself falling in love with Janice, seeing her every day for weeks, being drawn into her family life the way he had, and managed to make it sound as if Janice had pursued him, had made all the advances. He hinted that his father had pushed them together, then mentioned his father's pressure on him not to marry Lauren, vaguely wondered if maybe, perhaps, Charles Cornwell might not have something...? Oh, Lauren was wonderful, he said; she mustn't think he didn't feel that, she was a lovely girl!

But he wasn't, he said, quite sure, anyway, that they were suited, Lauren and himself; he wasn't certain she loved him, or he had ever really loved her, and maybe she felt that way too? She must have had doubts? Please forgive me, he ended, I really couldn't help it.

Lauren read the letter several times, and more and more a new picture of him emerged—a spoilt, selfish, rather weak young man who didn't accept responsibility, even for himself, but tried to blame everybody else for what he did.

Had that letter come out of the blue, as a total shock to her, she would have been quite devastated, but somehow having heard the news from Sam first had taken the initial shock of the blow. She was already over the worst by the time she read Rob's version of the facts.

All the same, she was in a state of depression and confusion for the rest of that weekend.

Her emotions swung like a weathercock: she wanted to cry one minute, and was angry the next, not least with herself because she had ever got involved with Rob Cornwell in the first place.

He had been right about one thing, though. She should have known from the start that it wouldn't work; there was too much against them and they simply weren't right for each other.

She felt she had been a fool. She had been in love with someone who didn't exist. She had loved Rob's charm, his gaiety, his warmth; she had loved his looks, his quick smile, the way his eyes crinkled up when he laughed. She had thought she knew him, but she hadn't. The man she had believed she loved did not exist.

She couldn't entirely blame Rob for that, though. She had been fooled as much by her own chemistry. Rob was intensely sexy; a very desirable man in more ways than one. She hadn't cared about his family background and money, but she had fancied him badly from the start, and had been blind enough to think that that was all that mattered. It wasn't. A physical attraction had no depth or lasting power; it wasn't love.

Rob couldn't be divorced from his family and their wealth and power, either, and he wouldn't want to be. Rob liked being a Cornwell, being important, having people stand aside for him, let him get away with murder. He wasn't ever going to settle for being just like everyone else.

There had never been any chance that he would marry her, she saw that now, too. He would have found some excuse, some other girl, if Janice hadn't come along. Lauren was simply not good enough, either for his father or himself.

So why had he ever asked her to marry him? A moment's impulse? To annoy and defy his father? Or had Rob too been fooled by a strong physical attraction?

Her thoughts went round and round, like a mouse on a wheel, until she was mentally exhausted. She didn't go anywhere that weekend; she stayed in her flat, eating little, unable to do anything much, just sitting around staring at nothing and thinking about Rob, wondering how she was going to face everyone at work on Monday. She hated the idea of people laughing at her behind her back, or, worse, being sorry for her.

Just before she left for work on the Monday morning, however, another letter arrived, a very different document; typewritten, formal, polite. It was from Charlie Cornwell.

Rob's father didn't mention Rob or the new engagement, or offer sympathy or apology. His letter was businesslike, telling Lauren that she had got the job she had applied for on the *Gazette* and could start there next month. It set out the terms offered and told her to get in touch with the personnel manager if she had any queries. Her contract would be in the post in due course, and meanwhile she could take the rest of the month off, and need not return to *Ultra*, unless she chose.

Lauren sat at the breakfast table staring at the letter and laughing with tears in her eyes.

Charlie Cornwell might not have offered sympathy, which could only have been insincere anyway, since he had not wanted her to marry his son—but she couldn't help feeling grateful.

He had handed her what she had wanted for so long, a transfer to a newspaper. It might be a consolation prize, but she wasn't going to turn it down because of Charlie Cornwell's motives, and at least she wouldn't now have to go into the office and face everyone there.

She hadn't expected such generosity from Rob's father, who had been hostile to her for so long. Pre-

sumably this was the generosity of the victor; Charlie
Cornwell could afford to be open-handed with her
now that he had won, but, all the same, it was sensitive and thoughtful, and she was surprised by it.

She rang Annie, who was already at her desk, and
knew all about it. 'I've heard your engagement is off!
I'm very sorry, Lauren,' she said gruffly, a tone of
voice that told Lauren she meant what she said. Annie
always got cross when she was upset; she had more
sensitivity under her tough exterior than people realised, but she wasn't good at being gentle and soothing. She felt badly for people, and angry because she
couldn't do anything.

'Thanks,' Lauren said, her face tight and her voice
offhand. 'But I'll survive, I expect.'

'I'm sure you will!'

Annie cheered up, relieved that Lauren wasn't going to be a crybaby and spoil Annie's day by making
her feel even sorrier for her. 'He was a pretty boy, but,
let's face it, no great brain—you would have got tired
of him, you know!' she said confidentially. 'Any intelligent woman would! And you're very bright indeed, much too good for someone like Rob Cornwell.'

Startled by the compliment, Lauren thanked her.
'Nice of you to say so! I suppose you heard about it
from Mr. Cornwell?'

'Yes, Charlie told me. And that you were going,
which I'm furious about!' Annie's voice sharpened—
she meant that. She had forgotten now that only a
short time ago she had been fretting in case Charlie
Cornwell took her magazine away from her and gave

it to Lauren. 'Are you quite sure you want to go to the *Gazette*? If I'm going to start a new magazine, I was relying on taking you with me. You're one of my best people. I could offer you a really interesting future, Lauren.'

'So you've come to terms with the idea of leaving *Ultra*?' Annie was a great realist, of course; it had been obvious she would accept Charlie Cornwell's terms, just as Lauren herself was going to do. He always sugared the pill—he was a clever operator and understood what made people tick. Lauren didn't like the man, but she had a sneaking respect for him as a newspaperman. He knew his business.

He knew Annie too. What would she come up with next? wondered Lauren. She would watch with great interest from the *Gazette*, but she wasn't staying on to find out. She had had enough of the magazine world.

'Well, I have had some exciting ideas,' Annie admitted cautiously. 'Early days to talk about them yet, but in a few months I may be in a position to make a definite proposition, Lauren. Stay with me and tell Charlie to keep this job on the *Gazette*.'

'Thank you, Annie, I appreciate the offer... but I want to work on a newspaper, you see. I'm sorry——'

Annie sounded impatient, annoyed. 'OK, have it your way, but keep in touch—if you change your mind later, ring me.' She paused, then said, 'I'm going to miss you. God knows who I'll find to replace you. Charlie said he was making the move immediate from today, but wouldn't you rather work? Keep your mind off things?'

Lauren heard the hopeful note in her voice and smiled wryly. 'Sorry, Annie, no, I'd rather not.'

She didn't explain why, but Annie must have known she didn't want to face a lot of kind, or unkind, comments from everyone on the magazine, and didn't argue.

'I suppose not,' she said with a sigh. 'Well, there's a lot to do—I'd better go. Will you be popping in some time to clear your desk and tidy up? Put your head round my door to say goodbye, won't you? And good luck, Lauren. Don't forget to keep in touch.'

Lauren went out an hour later, and, after long discussions with the local travel agent, booked herself a cruise to the Bahamas from Miami in Florida; a holiday package which included the price of an air ticket to Miami. It would use up a lot of her savings account, but at this precise moment she didn't care about that; she just wanted to get away from London for a while, as far away as possible. She had never been to either the Bahamas or Florida, so it would make an interesting trip. She couldn't wait to see the blue Caribbean.

She had to go into the *Ultra* offices once more to collect all her possessions and clear her desk, but she deliberately chose lunchtime, when there were few people about, and managed to slip in and out without talking to anyone she knew well. One or two people saw her and waved, gave her curious looks from a distance, but nothing more. Even Annie wasn't around; she was on a long lunch hour with a famous, and very sexy male film star whom she was interviewing for the magazine. Annie always kept the plum jobs for herself.

Lauren wrote her a note and left it on her desk, then hurried away. It felt very strange to be leaving *Ultra* so quietly. She had spent so long trying to get another job without succeeding, and now that she had got her transfer to the *Gazette* it was all somehow very hole-and-corner, almost furtive. She had crept in and out of the office as if she had something to be ashamed about, to cover up; as if she was the guilty party!

Climbing into her car, she looked at her own reflected face in the driving mirror. Why should you feel guilty? she accused herself. It isn't your fault you were jilted!

She turned on the ignition irritably. She would be talking to herself all the time next!

At that moment somebody rapped sharply on her window, and she jumped, her head swinging.

Sam Hardy was leaning on her car roof, looking in at her. He was casually dressed in well-washed faded blue jeans and a thin blue sweater, a faint dark shadow along his jaw as if he hadn't shaved that day. He ought to have looked disreputable and seedy. To her irritation, he managed to look very male, but elegantly sexy, and her teeth met.

She was tempted to ignore him and drive away, but that might have seemed like an admission that he disturbed her, so she wound her window down but left her engine running, hoping to give the impression that she had no time to chat.

'What do you want? I'm in a hurry.' She deliberately made her voice remote, unfriendly. He needn't think that she had forgotten what had happened in her flat on Friday night. She was going to keep the resolution she had made then—she was avoiding Sam Hardy from now on.

'I just heard about the job,' Sam said, his mouth grim. 'Did Charlie offer it to you—or was it your price for keeping quiet and not rocking the boat?'

Lauren flushed at something contemptuous in his voice. 'I don't go in for blackmail!'

'No? The other night you talked about something very like it!' His grey eyes had the glitter of polished steel, and she felt a nervous quiver run down her spine. Sam Hardy could be a tough opponent to face, but she was angry to think that he believed her capable of blackmail. Lauren would never have stooped to such a thing.

'I did nothing of the sort!' she snapped back, and Sam's eyes raked her face scornfully.

'Oh, yes, you did. You said you were going to sell your story to a rival paper. So what did you actually do? Threaten Charlie with reading all about his family secrets in another newspaper—unless he gave you the job you wanted?'

'No!' Lauren was so angry that she was trembling.

Sam's black brows arched coldly. 'No? Well, I don't suppose you would admit it.' He straightened as if to walk away, and Lauren threw open her car door, almost hitting him. He jumped sideways, his face startled.

She got out, her bag in her hand, undoing the clamp and then reaching inside with shaky fingers for the letter she had got from Charlie Cornwell.

'I got this today, but look at the postmark!' she bit out, and Sam took the envelope, frowning, gave the postmark a glance, looked at her briefly, his face tight, then skimmed through the contents.

'As you see, that was posted on Thursday, before I had an inkling that Rob was going to jilt me!' Lauren said bitterly. 'It just took all weekend to get to me!' She snatched the letter out of Sam's hand and got back into her car, slammed the door again and without another word put her foot on the accelerator and shot away.

Sam stood there like a statue, staring after her. She caught a brief glimpse of him, his face set and dark, then she was out of sight and driving in thick traffic which demanded all her attention.

She was flying to Florida next day, so she had some shopping to do before she went home. She felt she needed new beach wear. Feeling reckless, she bought a very brief and daring black and white bikini and white espadrilles, a pretty, sleeveless off-the-shoulder green sundress and on impulse a charming summer evening dress to wear for dancing on the ship.

She called in at the bank to pick up currency she had ordered. US dollars to spend on the ship and in Florida and the Bahamas. She was flagging a little by then; it had been a busy day and her row with Sam

Hardy hadn't helped. Every time she thought about the cutting edge of his voice when he accused her of blackmailing Rob's father in order to get this new job she felt rage flaring inside her. She had never hated anyone before; it was a draining experience. It occupied the attention far more than love ever did.

At last she got back to her flat, had a cup of tea and a slice of toast, which was all the food she felt she could force down, checked on her passport and finally packed her suitcase.

She had just finished doing that when the phone rang. She picked it up warily. 'Hello?'

'Lauren, I'm sorry,' Sam's deep voice said.

She slammed the phone down. She hadn't taken two steps before it began to ring again. Lauren took it off the hook, laid it on the table and walked away. A few minutes later she came back, replaced the phone and before it could ring again switched on her answering machine. Let Sam Hardy talk to that for the next fortnight, while she was away.

She had written to her parents to tell them where she was going, and give them the news of her broken engagement, but they wouldn't get the letter until tomorrow morning at the earliest, so she did not expect any important calls tonight. She left her answering phone switched on and went to bed early. She had to get up at six.

Somebody began ringing her doorbell an hour after she had gone to bed. She was still awake, so she padded silently along the corridor to peer at her caller through the little spyhole in her front door. It was Sam

Hardy, in a dark suit tonight; a very different Sam Hardy, his tall, lean figure formally clothed, white shirt, dark blue silk tie, and that smoothly tailored English wool suit. He was carrying roses; pure white ones with long stems.

Lauren stared for quite a while, knowing he couldn't see her eye looking at him through the fish-hole lens of glass.

He stared back, as if he could, his dark brows jerking together. His arm came up, his long-fingered hand stretched out to ring the bell. Lauren turned away then and padded just as silently back along the flat hallway into her bedroom. She got into bed and put her pillow over her head so that she couldn't hear the bell ringing.

Why had he come? Just to apologise? Or had he thought that she might be at an even lower ebb than she had been on Friday night, so unhappy and sick of her own company that she might weaken and he might finally get her into bed? She could believe anything of him.

She was going on this cruise for a number of reasons: to get away for a while, escape all questions and comment, and of course, for all the usual reasons for taking a holiday, to get some sunshine, see new places, relax away from everything familiar. She was not going in order to meet men, though!

The male sex was half the human race and it seemed a pity to cut them off completely, but from now on Lauren meant to treat them in a very new way. She was never going to trust a man again, or let him matter.

Oh, she would date anyone she fancied, have fun, but she was never going to care about any of them; she was never going to give any man the chance to hurt her.

When she walked away from Sam Hardy she had done so to escape any possibility of getting hurt, only to walk blindly into a new trap by falling for Rob and trusting him, believing he would never hurt her. He had, and it would be a very long time before she recovered from the shock of Rob's desertion, or of having Sam Hardy ruthlessly take advantage of it to try to get her into bed. In future she would treat men the way they had treated her.

Her cruise was everything she had hoped it would be; she had a tiny cabin to herself, but it was compact and very comfortable, and she spent most of her time out of it, anyway, enjoying all the facilities of the ship, which was nothing short of a floating luxury hotel. For the first couple of days Lauren kept discovering new places on the ship to visit: the hairdresser, the video-room, the massage parlour, the cinema, the gymnasium and jacuzzis, the swimming-pool, and, when she was in a more serious mood, the library or the computer room. She spent each day in a leisurely whirl of pleasure and activity: there was never a dull moment from sun-up until midnight. There were hundreds of other passengers, and since you changed your table at every meal you met a lot of them; had new faces to memorise, new jokes to laugh at, new life stories to hear.

Lauren was very careful not to overdo her sunbathing, kept her skin oiled while she was lying on her lounger on deck, and sheltered under a large sunshade when the sun was at its height, so that by the end of the first week she had a pale golden tan which looked wonderful against her sun-bleached blonde hair and slanting green eyes. It got her a lot of male attention, especially when she wore her black and white bikini.

Each time she dived into the pool on the upper deck, men's heads turned. She was well aware of all the stares, but she ignored them, mostly, and read a series of light novels while she sunbathed, listening to pop music on her personal stereo, which helped to distance her from those around her, and kept her eyes shielded against the sunlight by dark glasses which served a dual purpose. They kept out dangerous rays and made it easier for her to see, while hiding her expression from anyone who tried to force an acquaintance on her and got frozen off.

At other times she did talk to fellow passengers: in the restaurant, in the ballroom after dinner, when she joined in some organised activity like cards or deck tennis. She would dance with some of the single men in the evenings, even flirt with them lightly, exchange light-hearted chat while keeping them carefully at arm's length. She refused to be paired off with any of them, and she never let them make any advances.

'Are you frigid?' one young man asked sulkily, hoping to insult her, after she had slapped his octopus-like hands away.

'Totally,' she assured him gravely.

He looked quite dumbfounded, and Lauren walked on round the deck, half smiling. He was waiting for her when she came round again, his smile cheerful again. 'Well, how about a game of bowls, then?' he asked, and Lauren laughingly agreed to that.

But she had to get away, alone, sometimes; depression kept rolling down on her like fog, and then she would go to her cabin and lock the door, lie on her narrow little bed and let the gentle rocking of the ship lull her into a half-sleep.

When they began sailing around the many islands dotted around in the blue Caribbean, life became even more busy. Each day they sailed into a new port, disembarked, walked around some sleepy town or were driven around in an air-conditioned coach whose air-conditioning did not always work.

It was on one of these trips that Lauren bumped into someone she knew. She had grown bored with the shopping expedition their party had gone on, in yet another souvenir market, and while the others from the ship debated which T-shirt or piece of local pottery to buy she wandered over to admire the flowers on a nearby stall; a blaze of hot colour, orange and red and sun-yellow. A dark girl in shorts and bikini top, her eyes hidden behind sunglasses, was buying armfuls of flowers, and Lauren gave her a look of amused fellow feeling, since she would have loved to buy some herself. Only what on earth would she do with them on the ship?

Then something about the girl struck her, and she took a second look.

'Good heavens! Mel Lorenzi!' she exclaimed involuntarily, and the other girl gave her a horrified glance, then looked around with obvious apprehension.

Smiling, Lauren understood, also glanced around, then reassured her, 'It's OK, nobody heard me, and I won't tell anyone! We've met before—don't you remember? I'm Lauren Bell of *Ultra*?'

One of the current favourites on the top ten pop music charts, Melanie Lorenzi was only too recognisable, but perhaps she had hoped that, shielded by dark glasses, in this sleepy little backwater she could wander around without being troubled by fans. She wasn't exactly pretty, although she had a slim figure and good legs, and when she wasn't on stage the flame of her personality was doused, but when you saw her singing in front of a wildly cheering audience you knew what it was that had taken her up the charts so fast. She had charisma.

Peering at Lauren through her glasses now, she frowned, then gave a little exclamation and grinned, holding out her hand. 'Sure I do! Sorry, for a second I couldn't place you. Hi, Lauren. What on earth are you doing here. Don't tell me you've tracked me down?'

'No, I'm not working,' placated Lauren, smiling wryly. 'I'm on holiday, actually—on a cruise. Our ship called in here for the afternoon, although heaven knows why. There doesn't seem to be anything to do except buy T-shirts!'

'That's what I like about it,' Mel said. She was half Italian, half English, but had been living in the States most of the time for the last couple of years, because her work had taken her over there so much. She was in her early twenties, but she was already becoming an international singing star. Lauren had interviewed her a few months back, for *Ultra*, while she was touring Britain, and had liked her lively sense of humour and her down-to-earth attitude to her own fame. In fact, she remembered how Mel had talked longingly of getting away from it all on a desert island. Maybe this was the closest she had found to one?

'Are you on holiday here too?' Lauren asked as they both strolled slowly away from the flower stall.

Mel gave her a quick, wary look. 'Well…' She very obviously hesitated, then said, 'There's a quiet little café just around this corner—have you got time for a drink? When does your boat sail?'

Lauren looked at her watch and grimaced. 'Not for three hours! And I'd love to have a drink with you. It's so hot here—I'm parched!'

'Come on, then.'

They strolled around the corner of the square and sat down on the pavement terrace of the café, taking a table a little distant from the other handful of sleepy customers sitting under umbrellas and sipping their drinks.

'Is it a good cruise?' Mel asked after the waiter had taken their order and returned with their tall, iced drinks.

'I've quite enjoyed it so far.' Lauren sipped her cool drink through a long straw and sighed blissfully. 'Oh, I needed that.'

Melanie half drained her own glass and then leaned back, her dark eyes fixed on Lauren. 'You know, your article on me was the best anyone ever wrote about me. It was honest and fair, and I really appreciated it...'

'Thank you,' Lauren said, smiling back, touched and delighted. She didn't often get any sort of reaction from the people she wrote about, nor did she expect it. They were busy professionals, as she was; they probably never even read what she had written, but it was nice to know her work had been well received.

'You can imagine the stuff that some people write about me!' Melanie made an angry face. 'Utter rubbish, mostly; full of silly lies, and some of it nasty too.'

'My editor wouldn't want me to write that sort of piece. *Ultra* prides itself on being for intelligent women.'

'Yeah, I enjoy it, and I always look for your stuff. I think I could trust you.' Mel broke off, biting her lip. 'Look, can you keep a secret!' Her eyes searched Lauren's face. 'I had been thinking...well, that somebody should be there...from the Press. But we both wanted it kept secret, and we were afraid that if we told one reporter the others would all hear and come rushing down like wasps on a picnic! I actually did suggest you, I think you're different from the rest, I think we could trust you—but all the same...well, if I tell you, you've got to promise not to tell anyone about it until afterwards.'

Lauren's mind was working fast and furiously. She was already guessing before Melanie told her this amazing secret, but, as requested, she promised not to tell a living soul. 'I won't breathe a word,' she swore gravely, and Mel sighed.

'Thanks. Sorry to be so melodramatic, but we've both had so much hassle from the press, and it's very important to us to have a private wedding——'

'I knew it!' Lauren broke out, beaming.

Blushing, Mel said wryly, 'I suppose it wasn't hard to guess!'

'Not really. Are you getting married here, on the island? Is that why you're here? Who is he? Do I know him? When is it going to happen?' Lauren fired off excited questions, realising from what Melanie had said that she was going to get an exclusive story, scooping the rest of the Press. What a fabulous piece of luck, she thought. It will make a great start to my career with the *Gazette*.

Melanie laughed. 'Hey, slow down! You've made me breathless! I can't answer that many questions at once.'

'Sorry!' Lauren apologised, hoping she hadn't scared the other girl away. She badly did not want to lose this chance of a great story. If the editor and others on the staff, including Sam Hardy, suspected that she was getting her job with the *Gazette* solely as a consolation prize for having lost Rob Cornwell, it would at least prove to them that she was good at her job if she started off with a triumph.

'I didn't mean to babble! I'm just so fascinated,' she said eagerly. 'Are you marrying someone in the pop world? Will I know him?'

'He's not into music, he's an actor,' Melanie said, flushed and bright-eyed, took a deep breath and burst out with his name, her face proud and triumphant. 'It's Johnny Sefton.'

Lauren was stunned into silence, her head running playbacks of that famous face in some of the files she had seen. He had been beautiful when he began to act; a slender boy with gold hair and blue eyes and a slow, charming smile. He had shot to the top at once, and been there ever since; one of America's leading superstars. Far more famous than Melanie, he had been at the top of his career for nearly twenty years. He had also been married before, she remembered, a marriage which had ended in an acrimonious divorce some years ago, costing him a huge sum in alimony. Surely he must be close to forty by now? She had never read a word about Melanie dating Johnny Sefton! How had the two of them got together without the Press finding out?

Feeling Mel watching her with a frown, she managed to stammer, 'I . . . I'm sorry, you just took my breath away. Johnny Sefton! It's a name to conjure with! You lucky, lucky girl. He's my dream man, and I envy you, but I hope you'll both be very happy.'

'I hope so too!' Melanie muttered unguardedly, then said, 'Look, this cruise...would you mind very much if you didn't finish it?'

Lauren's eyes sharpened with interest. 'Not a bit! I came on it to relax and have some peace, and it has been peaceful...' She grinned. 'But I'm beginning to get bored out of my skull.'

Melanie laughed. 'Well, how would you feel about leaving the ship and staying here for the next week, to cover my wedding?'

Lauren did not hesitate. 'I'd be delighted!'

CHAPTER SEVEN

LAUREN rang the news editor of the *Gazette* three days later to warn him that she would not be appearing in the office on what should have been her first day there, the following Monday. 'I'm on to a scoop, a really big one! But if I'm going to get it, I have to stay here for a few more days,' she told him.

'What do you mean, scoop?' growled Freddy Grainger, a man she had met several times, on a casual basis, and remembered vividly as very big, very broad, and rather daunting. 'I decide who goes out on jobs in this office! Where are you, anyway? I thought you were on some cruise, and would be back by Saturday?'

'I was, but I left the ship. I'm in the Bahamas, a little island the ship visited. It's quite remote, no airfield, only ships calling in now and then... I'm staying at a villa— I met someone, I've promised not to tell you her name, but she's very famous, and she's getting married here, secretly, on Saturday, to someone even more famous. And nobody knows but me...' Lauren's voice rose excitedly and she was very flushed. 'And a few of their really close friends and family, and there won't be any other reporters here, not a photographer in sight, except one of the family, who's taking all the pictures, but I interviewed her for *Ultra* a while back, and when I bumped into her by sheer accident when my ship docked here for a few hours she offered me the chance to scoop the rest of the media!'

Freddy's voice sounded sharp and alert. 'Well, give me their names and——'

'No, I can't—I promised! That was a condition...they don't want anybody else to find out.'

'Good heavens, I wouldn't tell anyone! That would be the last thing I'd do. I don't want anybody else to get this story, any more than they do!'

'Maybe not, but you know that stories can leak out...what if someone at the paper decided to earn a few pounds by selling the story to one of our rivals?'

Freddy growled. 'Hmm...not likely, but I get your point. So where are you, exactly, did you say?'

'Staying at her villa.' Lauren had gone aboard the ship with Mel and packed all her possessions up, seen the captain, who protested about cruise regulations and problems with passports, finally managed to persuade him it was essential that she leave the cruise, and then had been driven in a horse cab through winding little streets up to the white villa Mel owned. She was ringing from the bedroom she had been given, looking out over lush green gardens full of pale trees and vivid flowers.

'Yes, but what's the name of this island?' demanded Freddy.

'I can't tell you that!'

'What if I need to talk to you?'

'I'll ring again on Saturday—that isn't long.'

'OK,' he conceded reluctantly. 'But don't forget to keep in touch!'

'Of course,' she promised, and rang off.

The villa was modern and very comfortable without being opulent; the rooms were spacious, marble-floored, largely white-walled, and not over-full of furniture, which was all very modern. Melanie had chosen deep couches and chairs covered with local cotton in strong, plain colours; red or yellow. The wood used throughout was local too—a dark reddish wood which glowed warmly when it was highly polished. Locally made woven mats lay on the floors here and there, and there were modern paintings on the white walls.

On the upper floor there were five quite large bedrooms; Mel slept in the main one, in a four-poster bed hung with gauzy curtains which kept away mosquitoes, and Lauren had been given this one, which also had mosquito netting draped from the ceiling above it. She had already grown used to sleeping behind this soft shroud.

She had been bitten several times since she arrived, which had taught her never to leave her windows open between dusk and the early morning, and then each evening before dinner she plugged an electric mosquito-killer into a socket in her bedroom, and by the time she went up to bed the room had a herbal smell and was free of insects.

Now, though, it was morning, the sun not yet at its height and dark blue shadows lying along the paths in the garden surrounding the villa. Lauren had been down to eat her breakfast rolls, made by Mel's housekeeper, and drink freshly squeezed local fruit juice and coffee. Now that she had made her call to the *Gazette* she meant to go down again to swim in the large, oval pool, then stretch out on loungers under umbrellas for an hour or two of sunbathing and talking idly to Mel. They had become friends over the past three days. Mel had been lonely and restless in the villa alone, and she was glad of some company.

Johnny Sefton hadn't arrived yet. He was sailing here, it seemed, in his own ocean-going yacht, pretending to be taking a leisurely trip around the Bahamas, in order to throw the media off the scent. He was due tomorrow evening, if the weather stayed fine and calm.

He was bringing most of the wedding party; his family, Melanie's, a few friends. They had flown into Miami, as Lauren had done nearly a fortnight ago, and boarded Johnny's yacht there. Other guests would be coming by boat from other parts of Florida or the Bahamas on the wedding day itself.

When Lauren joined her by the pool Mel was already in the water, her tanned arms lazily stroking along. Lauren dropped her white towelling robe on to the back of a lounger and walked to the tiled edge of the pool.

'Made your call?' asked Mel, treading water, and Lauren nodded.

'He almost died of curiosity, but I wouldn't tell him where I was, so your secret is safe!'

Mel laughed. 'Thank you—well, come on in! Don't just stand there like a great big magpie!'

Lauren laughed at this joke about her black and white bikini, rose on her toes, her arms outstretched, and dived in smoothly.

They were fast becoming real friends. Melanie had needed someone to talk to and confide in while she waited for Johnny to arrive. Although she hadn't quite admitted it yet, she was nervous about her forthcoming marriage, that was obvious. She was crazy about Johnny, but she had natural fears about the future. There was that age gap, for a start, and Johnny had one failed marriage behind him, not to mention some broken hearts.

Mel hadn't felt she could confide in the middle-aged secretary-companion who was the only person with her on the island. Joan Robertson had been hired by Mel's record company to act as her chaperon; to supervise the running of the house, answer fan mail, be a buffer between Melanie and the outside world. A tall woman with heavy-set brows and a muscular look, she could even act as bodyguard if the need arose. She had done all sorts of jobs, it seemed; been a typist, a nurse, a waitress, a barmaid, even worked in a women's prison. While she was there, nobody would harm Melanie, but she wasn't the type Mel could relax with, or ever regard as a friend, and Lauren's arrival had been a godsend.

Mel had spent the last few years touring around the world, moving from place to place; she had been lonely, bored, at times desperate for company and yet unable to let her hair down with anyone in case they talked to the Press.

Now she was starting to forget that Lauren *was* the Press! Of course, Lauren wasn't going to use all the private stuff Mel was giving her; she liked Melanie too much, for one thing, and for another the story she meant to write was going to be quite fascinating enough without using any of Mel's confidences.

'What about your family, Mel? How do they feel about you marrying Johnny?' Lauren asked as they lay on their loungers later, sipping cool drinks, and Mel grimaced.

'Mum's thrilled to bits, she thinks Johnny is fabulous, but Dad...' She sighed. 'Well, he's Italian, you know, and quite old-fashioned in his way. He keeps pointing out that Johnny is almost as old as he is, and has been married before. He's not happy, but he is coming to the wedding. Johnny's bringing them on his yacht. I hope it will give them time to get to know each other, but...' She broke off, sighing. 'I don't know how he and Johnny will get on, though.'

'And that worries you?' Lauren asked sympathetically, watching her. She had realised that there was quite a lot wrong beneath the glitter of Mel's career and marriage plans.

Mel shrugged. 'I'd rather my dad liked him, of course! I hate knowing Dad isn't happy about us getting married.'

'Maybe he'll change his mind, once he gets to know him?' suggested Lauren, and Mel nodded, smiling.

'Yes, that's what I'm hoping. Johnny's so wonderful that I don't see how Dad can help liking him, if he'll only give him a chance.'

The rest of the wedding party arrived dead on schedule, the following evening. Johnny Sefton talked to Melanie on his ship-to-shore radio telephone an hour before they docked, and she and Lauren walked down to meet them.

Melanie was wearing a vivid orange cut-off top and white shorts; she looked like a flame, her face excited, eyes brilliant, as she stared across the blue water.

Lauren had put on a blue silk sleeveless tunic top over white shorts. Her face, her arms, her long legs were now a smooth golden brown, her blonde hair attracted quite a few stares from the men lounging around on the quay.

They waited on the quayside, watching the dazzlingly white yacht sail towards them. Lauren was stunned by the size of it; it was like a small ship and must have a large crew to sail it. Mel had said Johnny didn't captain it himself; he wasn't qualified to do so, although he enjoyed working beside the rest of the crew, but Lauren hadn't suspected it would be quite this big!

She knew that after the wedding bride and groom were going to sail away in the yacht and spend their honeymoon cruising around this area, out of reach of the media. She had wondered if they wouldn't soon tire of that, but now she realised it would be heavenly.

At first the little figures on deck were like black dots, but gradually they grew larger and more distinct until it was easy to make out the shapes and faces.

'There's Johnny!' Mel said with a catch in her voice, and Lauren felt a strong sympathy for her. Mel was deeply in love, and it showed. Lauren fervently hoped she wasn't going to get hurt.

Johnny Sefton was leaning on a rail, waving; a slim, golden figure in crisp white shirt and shorts. Lauren had a weird sense of unreality, recognising that face and shape. She felt as if she had wandered into a film set.

A few moments later the yacht tied up at the quayside, the gangplank was lowered and Lauren and Mel went aboard. Mel ran straight into Johnny's arms, was lifted high, off her feet, and kissed. Everyone watched, smiling, feeling slightly unwanted, although the lovers seemed oblivious of their surroundings.

Lauren looked away to run a quick, interested glance over the guests Johnny had brought with him, trying to decide which were Mel's mother and father. The olive-skinned, broad-shouldered man whose black hair was greying? she wondered. Was that Mel's father? And the very jolly-looking woman with smiling eyes, whose features vaguely reminded her of Mel, and who was watching the bride and groom with such delighted warmth? Her mother?

Lauren looked past them, searching for people who resembled Johnny Sefton and might be his parents.

She heard the familiar whirr of an electronic camera; someone was taking photos of Mel and Johnny—

Lauren glanced that way, just as the camera was lowered. The photographer turned in her direction and began taking pictures of her. Her eyes met a pair of familiar icy grey ones, over the camera, and she did an appalled double-take. It couldn't be! Not him. Not here.

For what seemed an eternity she couldn't see or hear anything else; the shock of suddenly seeing Sam Hardy, when he was the last person she expected to see, freezing her into stone.

Then sound and sight came back. Sam stopped taking pictures and took a couple of long-limbed strides towards her.

Breathlessly, she muttered, 'W—what on earth... are you doing on board?'

'Well, I'm not the bridesmaid!' Sam bit out. His narrowed eyes wandered down over her, taking their time to assess her bare, golden-skinned arms and throat, the rise of her breasts under the thin silk top, the smooth tanned thighs and legs.

She flushed angrily under the taunt of that stare. 'Did you know I was here?' she asked, hoping to distract him.

'Of course,' he drawled, his stare rising to take in her face.

'But...how...?' Lauren couldn't hold his gaze; her green eyes shifted restlessly, and that disturbed her too, because there was no reason why she should be the one to look away when it was Sam Hardy who should be feeling guilty. He had tried to take advantage of her vulnerability when Rob jilted her. He should be flushing and stammering, not her! But he wasn't. He was hard and cold and impervious, like the marble floors in Melanie's villa—and, if she had any sense, she would walk all over him! But instead she was jumpy and breathless, every nerve in her body flickering.

'When you rang Freddy Grainger, you told him you'd jumped ship in the Bahamas, didn't you?'

She nodded, frowning.

'Freddy rang the shipping company and they told him where you'd left the ship.' Sam gave a shrug, his wide shoulders moving gracefully. 'It was that simple, and I'm sure you must have subconsciously realised he'd be able to track you down.'

'I just didn't think,' she muttered, feeling like kicking herself.

'You rarely seem to!'

The sarcasm made her teeth meet. She gave him a furious look which made no impact on him at all. 'I still don't see how you guessed it was Johnny getting married—I didn't mention him, or Mel! That was part of my deal with her. And how did you get on board his yacht?'

'I flew to Miami that morning, and some of these people were on my plane from London—I saw Johnny meeting them, last night, and overheard what was being said. It didn't take the brain of an Einstein to work out that Johnny was getting married—and I'd met him before, I knew him. I went up to him and had a chat, told him how much I knew and asked if I could take the wedding photos, and once he was sure no other Pressmen were lurking around he agreed to bring me.'

'I don't see why Freddy had to do all that detective work!' Lauren said with resentment. 'Why couldn't he just leave me to do the job alone? Why send you?'

'I'm a better photographer,' said Sam with breath-taking self-assurance. 'And this is essentially a picture story! Weddings always are!'

'Lauren!' Mel appeared beside them at that moment, tugging Johnny Sefton by the hand in her wake. They had been occupied with their other guests until then, hugging and kissing parents, relatives, friends. Mel was radiant. 'This is Johnny,' she said huskily. 'Darling, this is Lauren, and we can trust her, can't we, Lauren? She's going to write a lovely story about our lovely wedding!'

Lauren smiled at that famous face, holding out her hand, and Johnny slowly clasped her fingers, studying her with those incredibly familiar, very clear, very bright blue eyes. He was still beautiful, even if the new-minted look had gone from his features; time and dissipation had blurred the edges of his profile and softened the lines of his face, but she knew why he made Mel's heart stop every time she looked at him.

'I hope Mel's right,' he said, in the classy New York voice she recognised as well as she did his face. 'I hope we can trust you not to put the knife in—or hold us up to ridicule and contempt.'

'You can read my copy before it goes to the printer and decide whether or not you want the story published,' she offered impulsively, and caught the frown on Sam's face. He didn't approve of that, and nor would Freddy Grainger, but Mel had made her a friend, and Lauren didn't want to write anything about these two lovers that hurt them. She had been hurt herself, far too recently for the sting to have gone yet, and she felt a strong sympathy for Johnny and Mel.

Mel beamed, pressing Johnny's arm close to her side, and he smiled too, relaxing. 'Why, thanks, I'll take you up on that! We'll be spending our wedding night on the island and only sailing next morning, so there'd be time for you to write your story before we left.' He grinned, suddenly boyishly wicked. 'So long as you don't drink too much champagne at the reception?'

'I won't,' she promised, and then Johnny introduced Sam to Mel, and Sam explained exactly how he had come to be at Miami airport when Johnny met his other guests, how Freddy had found out where Lauren had left the ship.

Lauren apologised for such a silly slip, but Mel shrugged understanding. 'It wasn't your fault. I can see how it happened—never mind. Let's just hope nobody else finds out!'

'Come and have a drink before we go ashore,' Johnny invited, so Sam and Lauren joined the rest of the party in the long, luxuriously fitted saloon to have a glass of champagne, and then they all left the yacht and were driven in the waiting horse cabs, either up to Mel's villa, or to the island hotel, which had been entirely taken over for the wedding party. The reception was being held there after the wedding, and most of the guests would stay there. Only the close relatives were staying at the villa. Lauren had already moved her belongings down to the hotel that afternoon.

'We'll see you all at dinner, later,' Mel and Johnny told everyone who was staying at the hotel, waving goodbye to them.

People milled about, clamouring for the attention of the harassed desk clerk, who was on his own. The luggage was coming along behind, in the hotel bus. Sam Hardy was personally looking after his heavy camera cases and boxes of film. He didn't trust anyone to take as much care of them as he did.

While he was busy with his boxes and the rest of the party registered and were handed their keys, Lauren slipped into the lift and went up to her room. She needed to get away from everyone, particularly from Sam.

She bolted her door and went out on the balcony, which faced the harbour. The sun was falling like a blood-red orange into the sea on the dark blue horizon; streaks of flame ran on either side of it, making a dramatic background for the palm leaves and bougainvillaea that grew in the hotel gardens.

She could see Johnny Sefton's white yacht at mooring on the quay. A cluster of little boys were swarming, barefoot, up the thick ropes holding the yacht; the crew were leaning on the deck, watching them with amusement.

Lauren sighed, lifting her gaze to the darkening sky again. How quickly night fell here, and how beautiful this view was! She suddenly heard Sam's voice close by. He was being shown to his own room by the manager. Lauren listened idly, then stiffened. He was in the room right next door to hers!

Coincidence? Or... had he asked for that room? A hot flush ran up her face and she hurried off the balcony into her room.

She wouldn't put anything past him! She would make quite certain she locked her balcony doors tonight! She closed them now, before switching on the light in her room; she didn't want the room filled with insects. As she pushed home the bolt she saw Sam walk out on to the balcony of his own room and turn his head to stare, hearing her bolt her door. A mocking smile curled his lips, and Lauren shot away from the window, out of sight.

Oh, how could Freddy Grainger do this to her? If he had to send a photographer, why did it have to be Sam Hardy?

Of course, Sam was the best they had, she couldn't deny that. Maybe even the best anywhere? It could be argued; she was sure Charlie Cornwell thought so. He thought Sam was the jewel in his crown; he had gone on public record with his views. Certainly Sam had won enough awards!

But Lauren wished Freddy hadn't dispatched him after her, all the same. He reminded her of things she preferred to forget, and he made her uneasy.

She had just begun to get over the shock of being jilted; had stopped feeling like crying, even stopped being angry. She had almost stopped thinking about

Rob too. Whenever his face did turn up in her mind, she impatiently dismissed it. She didn't want to remember Rob or her brief engagement, or... She bit her lip, but had to admit it. Most of all, she didn't want to remember the way Sam had acted that night in her flat.

Her feelings were still, it seemed, in chaos. She didn't know what she felt about either man. She sometimes wondered if she had ever really loved Rob, for instance. Oh, she had found him very attractive; Rob was so good-looking and had enormous charm. She had enjoyed being with him, being seen with him. Other people stared so; she rather liked being envied by other women because she was with one of the most eligible men in London. The glamour Rob carried around with him had dazzled her, although she had lied to herself about that for a long time, preferring to believe it wasn't true.

It wasn't his money she coveted; nothing so simple. She had simply had her head turned by all that attention.

Had she ever been in love with Rob, though? She increasingly doubted it. If she had really loved him she wouldn't have stopped overnight, even when he broke off their engagement. She wouldn't be recovering so rapidly, learning so soon to forget him.

And she certainly wouldn't have found Sam Hardy so overwhelming when he made that pass at her.

She sank on to her bed and put her hands to her hot face, over her eyes. She had so very nearly let him seduce her. She had wanted him badly; the memory had power over her now, made her whole body ache and burn. When she stopped seeing him, ending their brief relationship, he had left some barb beneath the skin, a buried frustration, which kept tormenting her, even though she didn't trust or like him any more.

Oh, she must stop thinking about him! She leapt up angrily and went into the bathroom to shower and change for dinner. If she was going to see much of Sam Hardy while they were on the island, she was going to need all her wits about her. He was not getting within a foot of her again!

She waited to go down to dinner until she heard voices and footsteps on the stairs, and went downstairs with a handful of Mel's music business friends, who greeted her with intrigued curiosity.

'I thought Mel and Johnny didn't want any Press at the wedding,' one of the young men said after she introduced herself.

'Mel decided there ought to be one token reporter.' Lauren smiled. 'So she invited me, because I'd already interviewed her and she liked what I'd written.'

'Fair enough! And I bet Johnny didn't argue either, once he'd had a look at you!'

She wasn't sure she liked that joke much; if Mel heard it she might be hurt, and she gave the humourist a second, frowning look.

He waved her past him into the bar, where the rest of the party had gathered. 'I'm Stu Worsley, by the way,' he told her.

'The drummer?' she said, impressed. He was one of a popular group called Billboard Jungle. She wondered how many other famous people were here; fame did not always make your face immediately recognisable, although some of these faces were very well known.

'That's right, darling.' He mimed a drum-roll, grinning. 'Let's have a drink; I'm one drink below par. What can I get you?'

'A lemonade, please. I have to keep a clear head— I'm working, remember.'

'Boring!' he said, grimacing, and slid away to get her a drink. Some other young men closed in at once, their eyes flicking over her slender figure in the simple white silk tunic she was wearing.

'Very classy!' one of them flattered, and Lauren thanked him, eyes demure.

'Here, I saw her first!' Stu Worsley said, reappearing, a glass in each hand, shouldering his way through the little circle around her. 'Here you are, darling.' He put one glass into her hand.

She sipped and knew immediately that he had spiked her lemonade with something; gin or vodka, she suspected.

He grinned at her frown. 'Don't be a party pooper! One little vodka won't hurt you.'

Lauren didn't drink any more of it, nor would she accept a drink from anyone else. She took the glass back to the bar and got herself a bottle of orange juice, which she poured into a clean glass. Stu Worsley gave her an irritated look.

'No sense of humour, some people!'

By the time Sam put in an appearance, she had managed to talk to quite a few of the other guests. She couldn't make notes, but she had a good memory, and when she got up to her room she would jot down names and anything they had said that was worth quoting. They all knew she was a reporter, here to cover the wedding, so they couldn't object—and anyway, she wouldn't use anything that could cause offence.

Stu Worsley stayed by her side the whole time, watching her. He was a thin livewire of a man; around thirty, with spiky black hair and black eyes that moved restlessly over her, making her uneasy. She had the feeling she wouldn't like what he was thinking, if she knew!

'Oh, there you are!' a deep voice said behind her suddenly, making her stiffen, and Sam's arm went round her waist in a possessive gesture that she resented. 'I want a word with you,' he added, then looked at Stu. 'Would you excuse us, please!'

Stu scowled, but Sam didn't wait for him to argue, he just whirled Lauren away, out of the bar, into the empty foyer of the hotel.

'What do you think you're doing?' Lauren exploded resentfully, breaking away from his controlling arm.

Sam looked grimly down at her flushed face. 'I thought you ought to be warned. Stu Worsley isn't a safe playmate. He takes drugs, and when he's really high he can be dangerous.'

Lauren wasn't really surprised to hear that; Stu's black eyes had had such a strange glitter, but she resented having Sam waltz in and snatch her away from Stu as though she wasn't quite capable of looking after herself.

'Thanks for the tip,' she said remotely. 'But don't manhandle me again or you'll be sorry. Next time I'll slap your face.'

'Try it!' Sam invited softly, and her hands curled longingly at her side.

'Don't think I won't, if you lay one finger on me again!'

He put out one long index finger and stroked it down her bare arm, his eyes mocking.

'Very funny!' Lauren was going to turn away, but his hands closed over her arms again; he pulled her up against him and his mouth took hers with lingering sensuality, parting her lips and invading between them, sending a wild spiral of desire through her whole body. She should have hit him, then, pushed him away, but the shock of it kept her still, made her weak-legged and helpless.

Her mouth clung to the heat and power of his lips; she slid one hand round his neck and held his nape, her fingers touching his skin hungrily. Emotion filled her, like the sea; endless, without limit. She moaned with pleasure, wanting him.

Then Sam lifted his head and dropped his hands, and she was free, swaying there, flushed and confused, trembling.

He surveyed her with grey eyes that gleamed and taunted. 'Well? Hit me, then!'

She was provoked by his mockery, furious because she hadn't been able to shut off that sweet, aching feeling, because the minute he touched her she had gone crazy, and he knew it. Her hand came up to slap his face, but he grabbed her wrist and forced her arm down again, laughing.

'Oh no, you don't! I kissed you, Lauren, because Stu Worsley was watching us and I thought it might persuade him to leave you alone if he thought you belonged to me.'

Lauren glanced sideways, frowning, and saw Stu Worsley's back, just inside the door of the bar. He was talking to some of the other guests, but as she glanced at him turn his head to flick a look backwards, towards her and Sam.

Angrily she snapped, 'I can handle Stu Worsley! You mind your own business, and stay away from me in future! I don't want anyone to get the impression that I belong to you.'

'But you're going to...' Sam said in a deep, husky voice, and walked away, leaving her breathless and terrified. What did he mean by that?

As if she didn't know! Sam had made himself only too clear—transparently obvious! He meant that he was still after her, following on her trail like a tiger that had tasted blood once and was determined to make his kill in the end. She had escaped him in the past, refused to sleep with him, but he meant to get her, however long it took. His pride was at stake; his precious male ego. He had wanted her, and she had refused him; he couldn't forgive that. He would use any weapon, any tactic, to get what he wanted. Well, she was warned now—she knew for certain that he was very serious, she hadn't been imagining things. Sam was not going to give up or go away until he had got her into bed. Then he would vanish, leaving her to cope with the after-effects of having given herself to him.

CHAPTER EIGHT

LAUREN woke very early next morning, and walked down through the hotel gardens to the pool to have a swim before breakfast. The sky was a milky blue, the sun not yet over the horizon, and the water was cold when she dived into it. She began to swim vigorously, to get warm again.

Dinner last night had been an ordeal. She had been seated next to Sam, but somehow Stu Worsley had managed to get the place on the other side of her, and during dinner he had made a nuisance of himself. He had made some pretty dubious jokes, had brushed against her breast in leaning over to take some bread, and later had deliberately run a hand down her thigh and laughed when she slapped it away.

He had only stopped after Sam leaned back and tapped his shoulder commandingly. Stu had sneered, 'Yeah?'

'Do you want your teeth knocked down your throat?' Sam asked pleasantly. 'Leave her alone, or you'll be eating with bare gums.

Stu pretended to laugh in scorn, but after that he had left Lauren alone. Her own reactions had been muddled. She had been grateful to be rid of Stu's attentions, but she was disturbed by the way Sam was publicly marking her out as his territory and taking on any man who came anywhere near her.

It was a pity there wasn't someone to deal with Sam the way he had dealt with Stu! After dinner, there had been dancing in the restaurant, to a small local band, and she hadn't been quick-witted enough to think of any reason why she shouldn't dance with Sam when he asked her. Sam danced well, he was graceful and lithe, but Lauren had been very stiff in his arms. The contact was too intimate; she had to fight to disguise how fiercely it affected her, but she was afraid Sam knew. His grey eyes had watched her with gleaming mockery, reading the flush in her face, the betraying pulse beating in her neck.

She had gone to bed early, to get away from him, and lain awake, reliving the touch of his hand, the slide of his thigh against her, the tormenting invitation in his eyes.

Deciding she had had enough exercise, she hauled herself out on to the tiled surround of the pool and wrung out her water-darkened blonde hair, turning to pick up her towelling robe.

Sam was there to offer it to her. She took a deep breath, not having seen him until then. Lean and muscled in his black swimming-trunks, he held out the robe and, suppressing her start of shock, she said huskily, 'Thank you,' and tried to take it, but he was determined to put it on for her.

Lauren didn't want an undignified fight, so she had to let him step behind her and slide the sleeves up her arms. He took his time, standing much too close, his hands leisurely and exploratory. Her teeth met. Much more of this deliberate provocation and she would scream!

'If you're going to swim before breakfast, you'd better hurry up,' she said pointedly.

'Plenty of time.' As he spoke his hands slid down over her shoulders and she stiffened as his fingertips brushed lightly across her breasts.

'What do you think you're doing?' she broke out in a shaky voice.

'Just tying your belt!' he drawled, picking up her belt and loosely knotting it around her waist.

'Will you please keep your hands to yourself?' Lauren swivelled and glared at him. It was water off a duck's back; he wasn't at all impressed.

'We're going to have to get together this morning,' he said casually, as though she hadn't spoken, and hot colour rushed up her face as she tensed in disbelief. Surely he didn't mean...?

'Why?'

Sam gave her a mocking smile. 'To plan our story, of course.'

'Oh,' she said, on a relieved breath, and he watched her expression like a cat at a mousehole.

'What did you think I meant?'

'Nothing,' she said hurriedly. 'Anyway, what do you mean...our story? This is my story. I was the one who met up with Mel and was invited to the wedding—you're a gate-crasher!'

'Oh, very professional!' Sam drawled dispassionately, and she bit her lip, admitting the justice of that.

'I just meant...don't try to run the whole show! Don't keep giving me orders!'

'I told you yesterday—this is a picture story; all weddings have to be told in pictures.' Lauren opened her mouth to protest at that and Sam put a hand on her lips. Her green eyes flashed; she felt like biting him, and Sam read it in her face, a glitter in his own eyes, a warming smile on his lips. 'Don't even think about it, Lauren!' he said softly, electricity sparking between them, almost visibly. 'Anything you do to me will have repercussions—and I give you fair warning, you won't like them!'

Her lips set mutinously and he looked amused. 'Now listen! We're all going up to Mel's villa today, for a buffet lunch in the garden—I suggest we walk up there together and discuss our plans on the way?'

'Yes, OK,' she agreed reluctantly. She couldn't allow him a chance to tell her new editor that she hadn't co-operated with him on this story.

He was almost absently fidgeting with the lapels on her robe, lifting them so that they framed her damp face, like a towelling ruff, then he let the wet ringlets of her hair fall softly through his fingers, and the intimacy made her shiver.

She pushed his hands away angrily. 'Can't you leave me alone?'

'No,' he said, and he wasn't smiling now—he was almost grim, his mouth a cruel curve. His eyes slowly moved down over her, and she shivered, as if he was

touching her. His lips barely parting, he whispered,
'No, I can't leave you alone, Lauren.'

She broke away and ran back to the hotel, not feeling safe until she was in her room with the door locked
and bolted.

Sam Hardy was becoming a serious threat to her
peace of mind, and the sooner she got away from him
the better. At least he couldn't do more than torment
her with threats while they were here with so many
other people, though!

She dressed in blue shorts and a striped pink and
white top, and went down to breakfast. The buffet table was groaning with food: cold sliced ham, cheese,
slices of fresh local fruit, golden and luscious with
juice, cereals in earthenware jars, jugs of milk, coffee
and fruit juice, rolls, butter and black cherry jam or
honey, and little honey cakes still hot from the oven.

Lauren had finished her meal before Sam came into
the dining-room. He was wearing a white shirt and
black jeans, and his hair was wet from his swim. One
look and Lauren felt her pulses beat like flame in a
high wind—and that bothered her even more.

How could she keep him at a distance when her own
body was betraying her every five minutes? She immediately got up to leave, but she needn't have hurried away. Sam was otherwise occupied at the
moment; he sat down at another table with two pretty
girls who had come in with him. They were part of
Mel's backing group, Lauren recalled, and they made
no secret of the fact that they thought Sam very sexy.
As Lauren walked out she heard them flirting openly

with him and her teeth met. Maybe he wouldn't bother her if he had other game to hunt?

That should have made her happier, but, contrarily, it didn't. She was in a very bad temper as she sat down on the terrace in the sun to write some postcards home. She was beginning to think she lived in a state of utter confusion, never knowing what she felt, or thought, drifting like a jellyfish on seas which took her helplessly where they chose without her having any volition or willpower of her own.

Sam came out to look for her half an hour later, and as she saw him walking towards her with that long-limbed grace of motion which made women turn and stare, she bit her inner lip, despising herself for what she felt. Every time she looked at Sam she felt this slow-burning desire deep inside her which had been lit for the first time years ago and which had smouldered on ever since, out of sight, even though she had tried to stamp it out.

Sam's hard features and lean, powerful body aroused her in a way no other man had ever managed to do, or perhaps ever would again. The way she had felt about Rob had been a pale imitation of it, and she had always known that, even though she had longed to convince herself otherwise.

But she had too much pride and self-respect to have an affair with him, only to have him walk away and leave her bitterly unhappy.

After all, it would be utter folly to ruin her life simply to satisfy a purely physical need. She would despise herself if she did that.

'Shall we start walking to the villa?' Sam asked as he reached her, and she nodded unsmilingly, getting up.

'Freddy's sure we'll get a whole page, by the way,' Sam told her while they walked down through the hotel grounds into the little town.

'Really?' Lauren broke into a smile. 'That means there should be plenty of room for both of us.'

'Exactly. Now, how much of the past are you going to use?'

She looked blank and he sighed.

'Are you going to mention bride and groom's past? OK, Mel hasn't got much of one, but Johnny...' He whistled, grinning. 'Well, we all know about Johnny's past.'

'I don't see why I need to bring it up!' Lauren said, frowning. 'Nobody else will have this story, so we won't be competing with anyone. Look, what is the real story here? Not Johnny's past, but the wedding between two very famous people, a secret wedding on an island paradise. I don't think that needs much embroidery. It will be a bombshell anyway. If we go on about Johnny's ex-wife or old flames, it will take something away from our big picture—the bride in her wedding dress, looking radiant, the groom looking at her...' Lauren broke off her excited words as she realised Sam was looking at her wryly. With defiant green eyes flashing, she put up her chin and snapped, 'Well, what's wrong with that?'

'Not a thing,' he said.

'Then why were you looking at me like that?'

'I was only thinking——'

'Yes?' she insisted when he broke off, his mouth twisting.

'How romantic you are,' Sam said, and she flushed to her hairline, falling silent.

She had never thought of herself as romantic, she had even prided herself on being down-to-earth, shrewd—perhaps just a little of the hard-boiled, cynical working journalist. In her job it did not pay to be too soft-hearted or gullible, certainly not to be romantic!

'But I agree with you in principle,' Sam went on coolly. 'We should stick to the big picture, and that's the wedding photo of bride and groom. Readers will want to see a small glimpse of the island too, so I'll take some shots around the town and the harbour. Then there are the famous guests... I'll snap off a few films of anyone I spot, and the picture editor can decide whose faces to use. And of course you'll have to supply copy to go with those pictures—some glowing prose about the island, some small talk about the guests, what the women wore for the wedding, who the men were with——'

'You don't have to tell me how to do my job!' she snapped. 'How would you like me to start telling you how to take a picture?'

He gave her an ironic look. 'Do you even know how to use a camera?'

'Yes!' she threw back, then met his eyes and laughed suddenly. 'If it's simple enough!' she admitted.

'Look, Lauren, we're here as a partnership,' Sam reminded her. 'I was sent here to cover this story too, and I've been at this game a lot longer than you have. I'm the senior partner in this partnership! Be honest—if you were reading the paper, wouldn't you look at the pictures first, and only read the story afterwards?'

She bit her lip, grudgingly accepting that, and he nodded.

'Exactly. Of course you would. And it follows that the words have to fit the pictures, explain them, doesn't it?'

'I suppose so,' she said with reluctance, sighing, and Sam halted outside the gates of Mel's villa, holding out his hand with a smile so charming that it made her heart turn over.

'Partners, then?'

'Partners,' she agreed, shaking hands, but thinking wryly that it was a very unequal partnership. Sam saw himself as senior partner, the one who made the decisions, who was in charge—and saw her as very much the junior partner, the one who did what she was told! But what point was there at this stage in arguing over his attitudes, when she agreed fundamentally on the overriding importance of Sam's pictures? He was absolutely right, that was the trouble. People did look at the pictures first; instinctively the eye was drawn to a picture. One picture was worth a thousand words.

All the same, she silently determined to make every word she wrote *count*. The readers might look at

Sam's pictures first, but when they turned to her story they were going to be totally involved by it.

As they walked up to the villa Mel came out on to the balcony of her own room upstairs and waved. 'Hi there! I'll be down in a second; just order yourselves a drink, and I'll join you.'

Lauren raised a hand in reply, nodding with a smile. 'OK!'

Sam was watching her. 'Is she a real friend now?' he asked shrewdly, and when Lauren gave him a sharp look, nodding, made a wry face.

'What does that look mean?' she asked.

'It isn't a good idea to make friends with someone you're going to write about,' he observed. 'It makes your job harder. You start trying to please them, instead of writing a good story, and the two aren't always possible. If your friend likes the story it's on the cards that the editor isn't going to! Take my advice— back off from Mel until the wedding is over.'

Lauren knew he was absolutely right. She had already realised that liking Mel had limited her ability to write frankly about the wedding, afraid of hurting or offending her, but it was too late now. Mel was a friend, and that was all there was to it.

'I can't do it,' she told Sam. 'I don't even think it matters, not with a wedding story. It's strong enough to stand by itself. I wouldn't want to write an attacking piece, or bring up the past.'

'Johnny's past,' Sam said drily, and she gave him an impatient look.

'We've been over this ground already! I thought we'd agreed how we'd handle the story!'

'We did, but I still think you're going to feel you have to wear kid gloves when you're writing, in case you hurt Mel's feelings, or lose her friendship—and that's unprofessional, Lauren. You know it is!'

Before she had a chance to snap back at him, Joan Robertson came out of the villa to greet them, her heavy-set brows raised at the sight of Sam. 'Hello,' she said, to him, rather than to Lauren, and smiled. Lauren's lips tightened. Even Joan Robertson softened for him, damn him! Joan said, 'Mel says to get you a drink—what will you have?'

'Something long and cool, and non-alcoholic,' Sam said, and Lauren said she would have the same. Joan nodded, and vanished, and they sat down in the deep-cushioned white wicker chairs scattered everywhere on the wide terrace that ran all the way across the front of the villa. A tall black girl in a red dress came out with the drinks on a tray, smiling at Lauren, whom she had got to know during her stay at the villa.

'Hi, Lauren. How are you? Is the hotel all right?'

'It's great, thanks, Olivia,' Lauren said, and introduced her to Sam. 'Olivia works here part-time while Mel is here, but she also has a little boutique in town.'

'Not T-shirts?' Sam teased, and Olivia laughed, nodding. She had a laid-back, casual, easygoing air—nothing seemed to bother her—and she was very pretty, with her big, liquid eyes, curly hair and wide, smiling mouth.

'And other things! I sell all sorts of stuff.'

Sam seemed interested in her, which didn't surprise Lauren, although it made her teeth meet. He was always interested in pretty girls. 'Who's looking after the shop while you're here?' he asked Olivia, who shrugged her smooth shoulders.

'My mother, or one of my sisters—it's a family business. It doesn't make a fortune, we all have other jobs, but we live above the shop and whoever's at home minds it for a while.'

She had put the drinks on the low wicker table, and Sam reached over to pick up his glass. He sipped the lime-coloured drink, his lids half closed. 'Mmm, I needed that! It's hot today.'

'It's hot here every day,' Olivia assured him, and then Mel arrived. Sam got up, his glass in his hand, and Mel smiled at him, then looked at his drink.

'I'd love one of those, Olivia!' she said, and, with a nod, Olivia discreetly slipped away.

Mel sat down between Sam and Lauren, in one of the wicker chairs, kicked off her espadrilles and curled her tanned, bare legs under her like a child. Sam had his camera slung around his neck; he coolly started taking pictures of her, and Mel gave a groan.

'Must you?'

'Take no notice of me,' Sam said. 'Pretend I'm not here!'

'Don't we wish you weren't!' Lauren said tartly, and he gave her a narrowed look.

'No fighting with me in front of our hostess, or you'll wish you'd held your tongue!'

She flushed angrily, and Mel giggled, looking from one to the other of them. 'Are you two old friends or deadly enemies?'

'Both,' said Sam, out of his chair now and still busy snapping her, moving around and behind her, taking pictures from all angles, including glimpses of the exotic tropical gardens, the massed bougainvillaea, the glossy shrubs and sword-sharp palm leaves, and the terrace itself, with its tall columns supporting the roof and laying black bars of shadow all along the floor.

'We see this as a picture story, mainly,' he told Mel, on one knee beside her to take a close-up of her profile. 'Do you agree? I want to photograph every aspect of the wedding, and this setting: your friends, your family, your home, Johnny's yacht. We want to give readers a real idea of your life here, as well as your wedding, and Lauren will pick up on the details in her copy, describe in words what I've photographed— and, of course, what you wear for your wedding, the designer's name, that sort of detail. Women readers love it, don't they? They'll want to know what flowers you carried in your bouquet, what food was served at the reception buffet, what your guests wore, who was there...' He smiled at her with that charm which made Lauren so furious when she saw it going out to other women. 'You get the general idea? Are you happy with that?'

Of course, Mel said yes, her eyes big and lustrous. Lauren saw she found Sam attractive—who didn't? Mel was madly in love with the man she was going to marry, but Sam still managed to make an impression, and Lauren watched, thinking it would make her miserable to watch that happening all the time, Sam bowling women over at first sight, almost without trying.

Johnny Sefton came down a few minutes later and they all sat and talked, then some of the other guests appeared, and shortly after that they all had lunch—a buffet lunch in the gardens of the villa.

The buffet was set out on the terrace, but they carried their loaded plates out into the garden and sat on deckchairs under the trees or under beach umbrellas, or by the pool, eating and talking while they were entertained by taped music from loudspeakers set under the terrace roof. The sun was hot, the sky that unchanging deep blue, the air humid, hardly moving the great palm leaves or stirring the bushes of bougainvillaea.

When she had finished eating, Lauren wandered around from group to group, talking to people; identifying relatives and friends and famous colleagues of either Johnny or Mel. She managed to get several very good interviews from people, interesting sidelights on the bridal pair.

Later, she began to feel sleepy; she leaned back in her chair and her heavy lids fell. She wasn't the only one. The atmosphere was distinctly soporific. All around her people stopped talking and yawned, lay back, eyes glazed. Sam was the only one wide awake; his camera never seemed to stop whirring as he moved about taking pictures. The heat never seemed to bother him, and anyway, he had more energy than was good for him, or anyone around him, thought Lauren, without needing to open her eyes to see him. She felt him there, sensed his every movement, as though her body were in symbiotic relationship with his, and found that disturbing, because this awareness of him seemed to be growing daily deeper and more insistent.

She wrote up her notes back at the hotel, before dinner, while Sam was busy in his own room developing his film to see what he had got. He had brought out all the equipment he needed and preferred to do his own developing on the spot, in case something had gone wrong, or he had not got quite the shots he wanted.

Lauren was in the bar with the others when Sam came down for dinner, and her heart turned over with a terrifying lurch as she saw him.

What's happening to me? she thought, looking down with a flushed face. I'm falling for him all over again, and I must be mad. It has to stop right now. I must keep away from him.

The wedding was next day, which gave her an excuse for going back to her own room immediately after a very light dinner of fruit and salad, pleading a need for an early night. In fact, she did go to bed, and slept, but she kept waking up from dreams of Sam which disturbed her even more.

She had bought herself a new outfit for the wedding, at Olivia's boutique. Olivia did not carry a vast range, but Lauren had found a peachy pink dress she loved, made in glazed cotton. The colour comple-

mented her tanned skin and blonde hair, gave her a
glowing look. She also bought a broad-brimmed white
straw hat, which had pink satin ribbons fluttering in
a long tail at the back, and wore her own white leather
sandals, and carried a white leather bag to finish the
outfit.

She knew she would have stiff competition. Some
of the women guests were going to be wearing expensive designer-label clothes bought especially for the
occasion in Paris or London or New York; they would
be sheathed from head to toe in all the glamour money
could provide, including some dazzling jewellery, and
Lauren didn't intend to let that bother her. The only
man here she might have wanted to attract was forbidden to her, was out of bounds, so what did it matter how she looked?

From the minute she went down to a simple
Continental breakfast of rolls and fruit and coffee, the
day whizzed furiously past. Sam arrived, ate a peach,
drank coffee, then they went to photograph the pro-
ceedings at the villa before dashing to the church in the
little town to catch shots of the bride and groom ar-
riving there.

Lauren found the service moving. Mel and Johnny
looked so happy and the simple little white church was
perfect for the ceremony, sunlight filtering in through
stained-glass windows and making rainbow patterns
on the whitewashed walls, and on Mel's full-skirted
white silk and lace dress. She had never been a beautiful girl, but she was beautiful today, the soft lace veil
giving her hair a misty sheen, her eyes huge and glow-

ing, her face quite pale with excitement at times. She was carrying roses and carnations; there were white madonna lilies on the altar, and the air was heavy with the fragrance of flowers.

Sam took the wedding photographs alongside the local photographer, who would be selling his pictures in the town, or to guests who ordered them, and who was beaming ear to ear, because he was working with such a famous member of his profession. This might be a small island, a peaceful little backwater, but even there Sam's fame as a war photographer had penetrated.

The reception began immediately after the service; bride and groom drove in a flower-decked carriage pulled by a white horse whose head was adorned with nodding white ostrich feathers, and the guests followed behind in other carriages, squashed in together, five or six at a time, the horses moving like snails through the winding, narrow streets. Little boys ran alongside, shouting and throwing petals, people stood in the streets, smiling and pointing, people hung out of windows above them, waving and throwing flowers.

'Wasn't it wonderful?' Lauren said breathlessly to Sam while they were dancing later, after the wedding lunch. 'I've never been to a wedding like it—it was a dream! I hope you got some fabulous pictures.'

'So do I,' he said. 'I shall have to go up soon to get them developed before it's too late to get something better if any of them turns out to have been wasted.'

'That will take you hours, won't it?' She didn't want him to go away and leave her with the other guests, with Stu Worsley and others like him. She had finished her work, all but the actual typing, and that wouldn't take long. She just had to type out her notes in time for Johnny and Mel to run their eyes over them before they left tomorrow. Tonight she wanted to enjoy herself, and if Sam left she wouldn't.

'Afraid so,' Sam said, watching her disappointed face.

'Can't it wait a little while?'

The meal had been delightful, the food good and the speeches quite funny, and Lauren had possibly drunk one too many glasses of champagne. She was light-headed, a little dreamy, even drowsy, moving swayingly in Sam's arms, her body leaning on him. She wanted to go on dancing in Sam's arms for hours.

'I wish it could,' Sam said wryly, and she watched his mouth move and ached to feel it touch her.

After that dance he slipped away to his room to start work on his developing, and the minute he had gone Stu Worsley moved in on her.

'Dance?' he muttered thickly, grabbing for her.

'No, thanks,' she said with icy emphasis, pulling away, and luckily Johnny Sefton noticed what was going on, and came over.

'May I have this dance with you, Lauren?' he asked politely, and she smiled.

'I'd enjoy that, Johnny.'

Stu growled a protest, but was ignored by both of them. Johnny danced gracefully, as one would expect, and Lauren enjoyed talking to him.

'Stu Worsley is pure caveman!' he said drily, and she did not disagree. His friendliness encouraged her to ask one question she hadn't yet dared ask either him or Mel.

'Do you and Mel plan to have a family soon, or will you wait a while?' She met his eyes and got cold feet, her voice faltering. 'Or am I asking too personal a question?'

'It's very personal,' Johnny said. 'But between you and me, we do want children, although we haven't made actual plans as to when. Mel feels we should just let nature decide. If we have a baby right away, we'll be happy. If we don't, we'll have one later.'

After she had danced with him, she danced with several people he introduced her to, and then saw Stu Worsley stumbling her way again, so she decided it was time to leave. She would start typing out her article in her room.

The hotel was air-conditioned, but it was a very hot night, and her dress was sticking to her perspiring skin by then. She took a lukewarm shower and then put on a thin blue-striped cotton nightshirt, and sat down at the portable typewriter she had borrowed from Mel. All the other guests were downstairs enjoying themselves, except Sam, so she wouldn't disturb anyone.

She was absorbed in her work when she heard a sound behind her and glanced round absently, giving a cry of shock as she saw the gauze netting over the open balcony windows being pushed aside. The dark figure of a man crouched there briefly before launching itself into the room.

Lauren leapt up, her chair fell over with a crash, but she didn't have time to run before the intruder grabbed her.

She screamed wildly, fighting him off, knowing there was little chance of anyone hearing her. The music of the party was so loud that it drowned every other sound.

In the struggle she and her attacker fell backwards; she found herself lying across her own bed, the man on top of her, breathing noisily, grunting with excitement as his hands ran over her writhing body.

'Got you at last...' he muttered, and his face came down on to hers, his wet mouth avidly hunting hers as she turned her head from side to side, screaming.

Her thin nightshirt ripped, he grabbed her breasts, and Lauren arched in horror, kicking and punching, feeling very sick. What if she couldn't stop him, if nobody heard? If he managed to subdue her and force her to submit? She redoubled her screams and her attacker tried to stifle them, his hand covering her mouth until she bit him, making him swear violently.

A second later he was dragged off her and thrown across the room to smash into the wall and lie there, groaning, in a huddle.

Sobbing and shaking convulsively, Lauren gave Sam one look of mingled relief and shame, feeling as guilty as if she had been to blame for what had happened. She held her torn nightshirt together with both hands to hide her bruised body from him, staggered up and pulled the bedspread off the bed, wrapping herself in it, without even looking at him.

Sam walked over to where Stu Worsley was scrambling to his feet. 'I'll sue your ass!' Stu spat out, back to the wall, hunched as if afraid Sam would hit him again. 'Touch me again and I'll... She asked me in, dammit... I know what this is, this is some set-up. Blackmail. I know those tricks; my lawyers will see you off, mister. I won't pay you a cent!'

Sam gave him a contemptuous slap around the face, quite lightly, his mouth a distasteful line. 'You're disgusting! Guys like you make me sick. I ought to beat the hell out of you, but what's the point?' He took Stu by the collar, marched him to the door and threw him out. 'If I see you near her again, I'll kill you,' he promised as Stu crashed to the floor.

Stu howled some vicious insults back, but as Sam took a threatening step towards him he ran, and Sam slammed the door behind him.

Sam turned towards Lauren, his brows black and his eyes angry. 'Are you all right?' he bit out, as if he wanted to hit her too.

'Five minutes later, and he would have raped me!' she said bitterly. 'Oh, yes, I'm fine!' What right did he have to look at her that way?

'You shouldn't have let him in!' Sam snarled back, and she was almost breathless with outrage.

'Let him in? I didn't let him in! He came in from the balcony, the way you did!'

'You should never have left your windows open!'

'It was too hot to breathe!'

They were standing there shouting at each other in a blinding rage, when what she wanted to do was fall into his arms and cry her heart out.

'You're a brute!' she said fiercely. 'I almost got raped, and you come along and bawl me out . . . as if I hadn't had enough shocks for one night——'

'It was a damned shock to me too, to hear you screaming like that, and not to be able to get in here as fast as I wanted to!' Sam bit out. 'All the time I was running I was imagining what was happening to you and going crazy . . .'

Lauren bit her lip, staring up into those glittering, dangerous grey eyes, silenced. She bent her head, shivering, because now that she had stopped shouting at Sam she was back in deep shock again, the shudders of fear running through her body and leaving her weak.

'Don't,' Sam said hoarsely, and his arms went round her, but lightly, as if he was afraid to touch her in case he frightened her again.

She would never be frightened of Sam that way, though. She knew what sort of man he was, and he was not the type to use force on a woman. She trusted Sam, and she could let herself lean on him, give in to the weakness creeping over her body. The sobs began to wrench through her again. She needed his warmth and security, and he sat down on the bed and held her on his lap, still wrapped in her bedspread, but cradled in his arms, like a swaddled baby.

He stroked her hair, and kissed her temples, her wet eyes, kissed away her tears with light, brushing kisses on her long lashes, kissed her nose, her cheeks, her ears, her jawline, before coming at last to her mouth, which was waiting for him, parted and breathing softly, hungrily.

'Lauren...' he muttered, taking her mouth, and the kiss was like a forest fire raging between then, consuming them both, blotting out the memory of everything else that had happened.

Minutes later, she struggled to free her arms, to slide them around his neck, to stroke his hair, caress his nape, and Sam laughed huskily, deep in his throat.

'It's like making love to an Egyptian mummy,' he said. Let me...'

His fingers delicately parted the wrappings and she put her arms round his neck, then her breath caught as she saw the way he was looking down at her body, laid bare by the torn nightshirt. She didn't try to hide it now, but lay there, quivering, feverish with desire, and Sam slowly bent his head.

She gave a wild cry as she felt his lips, his warm tongue gently caress the hard tips of her breasts. The pleasure was so intense that it almost hurt. Her fingers ran through his thick, warm hair, clenched on it in a spasm of almost anguished arousal, her eyes closing. She had stopped thinking and being sensible, being wary of letting him get too close. The closer the better—that was the truth of what she wanted. She wanted Sam closer than any human being had ever been to her before. Heat burned inside her, a strange dryness in her mouth, as his hands moved tenderly on her body.

'I want you, Lauren,' Sam said, as he had said before, and this time she admitted how she felt, this time she said it too.

'Oh, yes,' she moaned, her golden tanned body arching under the caress of his fingertips. 'I want you too, darling...'

He took his time, undressing, kissing her, lifting her on to the bed and joining her—and she knew from the way his grey eyes watched her, waiting for some sign, that he was giving her the chance to say no again, she could still say no if she wanted to. But she didn't. She couldn't have let him go, even if he had wanted to— she was going crazy, waiting for him, she had never wanted anything as much as she ached for the satisfaction his body could give her.

They made love in a strange sort of slow frenzy, like a drugged dream, piercingly sweet and ecstatic.

Lauren had denied her love for him for so long. Now that she had finally admitted it she felt her body spin out of all control. She hadn't imagined she could act that way; all inhibitions shed, making love with such abandonment and passion. The tension of desire had stretched to breaking point, it had snapped. She moved with him in that dreamlike dance, wildly, urgently, and at last she fell with moaning cries down through a seemingly endless spiral of satisfaction, hearing Sam groaning on top of her.

They were both so exhausted afterwards that they fell asleep in each other's arms with a sheet thrown lightly over them and the cool night breeze blowing in from the sea through the open balcony windows.

When Lauren woke the room was full of pale golden daylight, and for a second she didn't remember what had happened the night before. Then her eyes flew open as it all came back. She turned her head in a shy, uncertain movement, but Sam was not in the bed. Sam was not in the room. He had gone while she slept.

It didn't surprise her. She had discovered last night that Sam had a surprising sensitivity hidden under that tough exterior. Smiling, she slid out of bed and ran over to the window to look at the sea. The day was full of promise; she was happier than she had ever been in her life before. Last night, Sam had been more than a passionate lover—he had been the man she had always waited for, and she knew it had been like that for him too. He couldn't have made love to her like that if he had not felt the same way. There might have been lots of women in the past, but Lauren was certain that that was over. Sam loved her. He had said so, and she believed him.

She showered and dressed, finished typing out her story, and then went down to breakfast, expecting to find him waiting. She walked into the breakfast-room, her heart in her eyes, and found Mel and Johnny waiting, smiling back at her.

'Oh, there you are! You're up later than us!' they teased. 'Have you got your story ready for us to read before we leave? We've seen Sam's pictures, and they're wonderful, we loved them. The only problem was deciding which we liked best!'

'Oh, that's terrific!!' she said happily. 'I hope you like my words as much as you liked his pictures.' She held out the folder containing her typed pages, looking around the room. 'Where's Sam?'

'Oh, he left an hour ago,' Johnny said casually, running his eye down the top page of her story.

Lauren went icy cold. For a moment her brain seemed dead, she couldn't think, let alone speak, then she said carefully, 'Left? For where?'

'Back to London, I guess,' Johnny said, without looking up. 'He wanted to get his pictures back immediately, and there's no facility for sending them back on the wire from this island. There was a plane going this morning from Bermuda, so he went there by helicopter and he should be in London by tonight, to get the story into the paper tomorrow.' He looked up, smiling at her then. 'Oh, I forgot—he left a message for you...'

'Yes?' she asked huskily.

'He said you should telephone your copy through today.' Johnny went on reading her story, and Lauren went on breathing, went on standing up on her two feet, but she was fighting to hide the anguish flooding through her.

Sam had got her to bed at last. He had never given up, he didn't like being beaten and was determined to get her in the end. It must be an obsession with him, to get his own way, a matter of male pride. Well, finally he had his little victory. She had been weaker, after all; she had not been able to go on fighting, she had given in, as Sam had always been sure she would.

He was the winner of their little duel, and now he had moved on without a backward glance, leaving her the way he had left all the other women who had briefly shared his bed.

CHAPTER NINE

LAUREN got back to London two days later. Although she kept telling herself not to be so stupid, she still hoped to find a message from Sam waiting, and when there wasn't her heart plummeted. It was late at night, she was tired; she went to bed in a fog of depression and slept badly, but she was getting used to that. She hadn't slept well for a long time, and she couldn't face food; her appetite was gone.

She began work at the *Gazette* next morning. It was the same building, of course, nothing new about that, but this time she would be working in the east wing, not the west wing of the building, and she got out of the lift at a lower floor. The newspaper was closer to the printing department, a stair ran from the newsroom down to the printers so that access was faster, and this sense of urgency and immediacy was apparent the moment she walked out of the lift. People moved faster, looked more absorbed than they had on *Ultra*, which was a monthly magazine where time was not so pressing, except on days when the magazine went to print.

Lauren walked slowly, staring about her, trying to get her bearings, and a few heads were raised from desks in the newsroom. Eyes observed, registered, exchanged glances. She was new, and the other reporters at once realised who she was—Lauren had arrived with a lot of advance publicity. Everyone in the newsroom knew all about her broken engagement, followed suspiciously by her being given a job in the newsroom here, and then this big coup she had pulled off, scooping the rest of the Press with the news of Mel and Johnny Sefton's wedding.

Rumour had said that she was a sexy blonde; the reporters in the newsroom that day were mostly men, and their speculative gaze noted her blonde hair, those slanting, misty green eyes, the slender figure and long legs. Rumour had not lied.

Lauren found Freddy Grainger, the news editor, in his private office, at the far end of the newsroom. He looked up from his desk and stared shamelessly, pursing his lips in a whistle.

'So *you're* Lauren Bell! Now I get it!'

'Get what?' She sat down in the chair on the other side of his desk when he waved a hand at it, and he grinned wolfishly at her, his yellowish eyes watching her cross her legs, her straight black skirt sliding up over her knees. She had dressed to be inconspicuous; the neat skirt, a demure white silk shirt, wide-lapelled and tailored to fit her like a glove, but it didn't seem to have worked. She was getting far to much attention, and this morning that was the last thing she wanted.

'Why you've been making the headlines!' Before she could ask exactly what he meant by that, he went on, 'Congratulations on your wedding story. It was good stuff. You and Sam did a wonderful job.'

A little flushed, she said, 'Thanks,' huskily. Was Sam in the office? she wondered. Would he appear at any moment? She found it hard to listen to Freddy; her mind was on Sam all the time. She didn't know how she was going to cope with seeing him again. No doubt he would saunter in, cool and at ease, and expect her to be as calm, but she had a disadvantage Sam did not have. She had a heart, and at the moment it hurt badly. Did hearts really break? Or did they just feel as if they had?

She kept her eyes down, cloaked by her long, blackened lashes, needing to hide the pain from Freddy Grainger. He was talking cheerfully. 'You make good partners, you and Sam— I might pair you up quite often in future.'

Lauren stiffened. The very idea made the blood freeze in her veins. Pair up with Sam? Quite often? She wouldn't be able to bear it.

'He's our top guy,' Freddy said. 'Best photographer we've got, maybe have ever had...'

She had heard that before. She frowned, tracking the memory down, and realised Rob had said it, repeating what his father often said. Maybe Freddy had heard Charlie Cornwell too? Their proprietor was God to the senior staff; they took all their ideas and opinions from him.

'Sam should have a good writer to team up with him,' said Freddy. 'I doubt if he'll be working abroad much in future. His war years are over, but I don't see him settling for a routine day's work. He's been talking about special assignments—something a bit different.'

Lauren stared blankly. 'Special assignments?' She couldn't think clearly, except to register that Freddy meant this—it might happen, she might find herself twinned with Sam and living with the daily anguish of watching him with other women. No, she thought. No, I couldn't.

'Yes, it's a great idea. They come up all the time, stories that are out of the ordinary, like that wedding scoop. We do need a crack team to cover stories like that, and I think it would work, having Sam cover them, but he'd need a writing partner, and I've been looking around for someone he could work with.' Freddy's eyes twinkled. 'Just between you and me, I wasn't having much luck. Sam can be daunting, but he was very impressed with you—so how about it? What do you think?'

She cleared her throat. 'Is he around now?'

'No, he's in Scotland, covering a train crash,' said Freddy, and Lauren felt her body slacken, the fog of depression come down again.

'Can I think it over?'

'Sure, let me know,' he said complacently, and she could tell he didn't believe she would refuse. Few women would turn down a chance to see a lot of Sam Hardy. Unless they had been badly burnt already and wanted to stay away from the fire!

Freddy took her out into the newsroom and showed her the desk she would use, introduced her to several other reporters sitting nearby, who were very friendly. She got her first assignment for that afternoon, covering the opening, by a minor member of the Royal Family, of a new department store in Oxford Street.

Lauren wasn't too happy about it. It began to look as if she was going to find herself specialising in social occasions, on the gossip side of the paper, when she had fought to get on a newspaper in order to cover news stories! She could have stayed on *Ultra* if all she wanted was to write women's stories! But how did she make Freddy take her seriously?

Patty came down the room half an hour later, while Lauren was reading through the newspaper 'Style Book', a thick tome which covered the rules of house style, from grammar and punctuation to methods of writing a story in the *Gazette's* voice. Basically, it was common sense and good English, but one or two of the rules struck her as old-fashioned and quite comic.

When Patty arrived in front of her she looked up, startled, and Patty gave her a sulky, reproachful look. She looked very delicate and wan, in a lavender sweater and purple skirt, her brown eyes underlined with dark shadow, as if she had been crying all night. 'What's all this talk about you and Sam?' she accused.

'What talk?' Lauren fenced warily.

'Oh, don't play games with me! You know what I mean. They say you're his new woman—is it true or not?'

Lauren went scarlet, then white; shocked and dismayed. 'Who says so? What do you mean...they?'

Surely Sam hadn't been boasting all over the office? It was true that his affairs had always become common knowledge, but she had supposed that that was because everyone saw him dating a certain girl, or the girl herself talked to her friends. It had never occurred to her that Sam might gossip or boast. But who else could have spread the story? Nobody else from the paper had been on the island.

'I notice you don't deny it!' Patty muttered, her lower lip trembling. 'Was he comforting you for losing Rob? I was sorry for you when I heard, you know. I thought...oh, poor Lauren, what a shame, how could he do that to her? And five minutes later you're off with Sam, after all the things you said about him! I suppose you wanted him all along, and were just being dog-in-the-manger. Well, enjoy it while you can. It won't last long.'

Lauren flinched, and Patty gave her a bitter smile.

'Yes, hurts, doesn't it? But you said it yourself, so you know I'm not just being a bitch, which is more than I can say for you!'

She walked away, and Lauren realised that everyone within earshot had been listening with fascination to their row. She had only been working there a few hours, and already she was giving her colleagues a lot of fun just eavesdropping on her life.

She was glad to get out of the office and go off to lunch in the wine-bar across the road before she took a bus to Oxford Street, but she had no sooner sat down with a plate of cold salmon salad in front of her than she realised that everyone in there was watching her, and whispering. The gossip about her and Sam was moving faster than the plague.

She was grateful that she had so many other things on her mind that week. It helped to have this new job, to have so much to discover and get accustomed to—she could always push thoughts of Sam to the back of her head and get on with her work.

He hadn't yet shown up in the office. Having covered the Scottish train crash, he was in the right spot to be sent on immediately to an oil rig off the coast of Scotland which had suffered in a savage storm.

Lauren did see Rob and Janice one evening as she was leaving for home. They were coming into the foyer, both in evening dress, which probably meant that they were accompanying Charlie Cornwell to some glitzy dinner party or ball. The two of them glittered with the aura of money and complacency; very sure of themselves, and pleased with their lives. They really were a golden couple, and perfectly suited—she could admit that now, staring. Janice was in a dress of glowing amber, diamonds at her ears and around her throat. She looked magnificent. Lauren herself would never have looked this good on Rob's arm. He was a beautiful sight too, in his smoothly tailored dark suit and immaculate white shirt; almost too gorgeous to be real.

It gave her an odd little shock. It seemed so long since she had seen Rob; a lifetime ago. She hadn't just been someone else, with other feelings. It had all been unreal, those months with him. She had shed him like a butterfly shedding a chrysalis; he had been the co-

coon within which she had hidden from the real thing, a love too intense for her to bear. She had been pretending she didn't love Sam, she had never really loved Rob at all, but now she knew the truth, and even though she was already suffering the anguish she had known would be the result of loving Sam there was no going back. She couldn't stop loving him now, or pretend even to herself that she didn't.

Janice saw her a second later, and stopped, raising her carefully pencilled brows. 'Oh, hello!' she said in her American drawl.

Rob turned his head, looking startled, frowning as he met Lauren's eyes. He didn't say anything.

Lauren did. 'Hello—how are you?' she asked them politely, sharing the remark between them with a rapid glance from one to the other.

Rob scowled and didn't answer, but Janice said eagerly, 'We're fine, and we keep hearing about you—and Sam! I'm so glad you two got together!'

Does everyone know? thought Lauren savagely. People around here have nothing better to do than talk about each other! When Sam comes back, and they realise he's already lost interest in me, they'll start commiserating with me, I suppose! They'll be embarrassed, sorry for me. Poor Lauren, they'll say... dumped twice in such a short time! How sad. It made her stiffen with outraged pride. She didn't know how she was going to bear it.

'We might have guessed it was on the cards! Sam Hardy is very good at moving in on women who are having a problem... like he did with Patty!'

Rob's voice was spiteful, and Janice gave him a surprised look, frowning.

'Darling, that isn't very kind!' She looked hastily at Lauren. 'I like Sam; he's a terrific guy.'

Lauren was amazed to find herself liking her; there was a sincerity, an open-hearted warmth, about Janice that she hadn't expected, and she smiled back at her.

'We must go,' Rob said in a sulky voice. 'Dad's waiting for us.' He took Janice's arm to drag her away, but she wouldn't budge yet.

'I must just tell Lauren how much I admired her story about Johnny Sefton's wedding! It was so well written, and of course Sam's pictures were beautiful. You did a great job, the two of you! Really moving. I do hope that marriage is going to last.'

'I hope so too,' said Lauren seriously. 'I think it may. Mel is such a nice girl.'

Janice nodded, her eyes warm. 'That came over in your story, how much you liked Mel. Well, liked them both. It was an exceptional piece, Lauren.' She paused, chewing her lower lip uncertainly, then said shyly, 'I hope...maybe...if it isn't too...well, I'd just love to have you and Sam write up my wedding.'

Lauren blinked, taken aback, and then Rob and Janice had gone, hurrying across the foyer into a lift without looking back.

What a nerve! Lauren thought, making her way home through a warm early summer evening. Does she really imagine I could cover her wedding to a man I was once engaged to? She must be as well armoured as a rhinoceros!

But when she had had time to calm down, while she was making her supper, she realised she was being ridiculous. She didn't love Rob, she wasn't unhappy over losing him. She didn't care whether he married Janice or not. In fact, she was beginning to think Janice was rather nicer than he was! He had been spiteful and unfriendly this evening; he seemed to be taking a dog-in-the-manger attitude over her dating Sam, and that was typical of Rob. He was the kind who wanted to have his cake and eat it. But Janice was kind-hearted and thoughtful. Sam had said so, hadn't he?

Well, why shouldn't she report their wedding? Oh, it might cause a little whispering around the building. People might grin, or be surprised. But who cared what other people thought!

Next morning when Lauren walked into the newsroom she felt the back of her neck prickle, all the little hairs on her skin rise up. She knew what it meant; her instincts were going off like alarm bells. Sam had to be here.

She sat down behind her desk before she risked taking a look down the long room. Sam was in Freddy's office, lounging on the edge of Freddy's desk, with folded arms, his back to her. She saw the morning light gleam on his black hair, took in what he was wearing, jeans and a cream sweatshirt. He looked so vital, alive... so unbelievably sexy...

Her heartbeat redoubled and she looked down, trying to regularise her breathing. Had he always done this to her? She was trembling, her skin burning, and Sam wasn't even within touching distance!

How on earth was she going to control this? She went through the contents of her in-tray, skimming over the agency tapes which all the reporters got, reading the items of mail which had come that morning.

All the time she was struggling to force her feelings underground, hide what was going on inside her. Sam hadn't even bothered to write, or ring, since he last saw her, on the island. He had just gone, left her, without a sign. Didn't that tell her all she needed to know?

He didn't care tuppence for her. All she had ever been to him was the one woman he had wanted who managed to get away, and he had been determined to get her, however long he had had to wait. Why was he like that? What drove him on from woman to woman? What had begun this obsession with notching them up, adding them to his score? Lauren had heard of men who collected antiques, books, paintings, and would move heaven and earth, pay any price, to add a rare item to their collection, but they didn't hunt out living things. Sam was a collector who didn't keep what he acquired, just moved on immediately to the next woman without looking back.

He was utterly ruthless about it; she had seen that too many times to doubt it, and if she didn't learn to wear a cool, indifferent mask whenever she saw him her life wasn't going to be worth living.

A shiver ran down her spine as she felt him walking through the office, towards her. She didn't look up, her eyes fixed on a letter she was pretending to read without having a clue as to its contents, fighting to get control of herself.

He halted in front of her desk, and she took a deep breath before lifting her head.

'Hello,' Sam said, looking into her eyes and smiling.

The charm twisted her heart, but she managed to stay outwardly calm, give him a polite smile. 'Hello.' Was that her voice? She sounded so normal. Nobody could tell from it what this was costing her.

There were other reporters at the desks all around them, listening and watching. She was aware of them, and, no doubt, so was Sam. That helped. If they had been alone she might not have been able to keep up that cool exterior.

'Can we have dinner tonight?' he asked casually, surprising her. She hadn't expected that. But maybe he meant to tell her over dinner that it was over, he was sorry, but he had met someone else. Or whatever he usually told his discarded women! Of course, he might have some compunction about dropping her so soon after Rob had. He might feel sorry for her—and that thought stiffened her backbone. She didn't want his pity, he could keep it!

'Sorry,' she said lightly, 'I have a date.'

'Break it,' he said, and that was what he would do, of course. Without a second thought.

Lauren smiled, shaking her head. 'Oh, I couldn't do that.' She was pleased with the sound of her voice; cool, distant, faintly amused.

Sam stared down into her face, his brows snapping together, his grey eyes taking on a glitter that told her he was getting angry.

'Sorry,' she said again, still smiling, although her teeth were aching. 'I have a lot to do this morning.' She looked down at the letter she held and saw that her hands were shaking. Somehow she forced them to be still, almost holding her breath, a pulse beating at the side of her mouth, aware of Sam standing there, seeing out of the corner of her eye the tension and threat of his body, of the clenched hands, the long, muscled legs in his blue jeans.

Then he swung away and strode off, out of the office. As soon as he had gone Lauren got up too, knowing that everyone else was watching her, and somehow managed to make it to the powder-room before the last of her energy ran out and she collapsed.

She shut herself in a cubicle and leaned on the wall, her face in her hands, trembling violently, tears burning in her eyes. Well, she hadn't let Sam see what he had done to her, she was sure she had fooled him—but at what cost!

It was ten minutes before she could return to the office, her hair brushed smooth, her face cool again, her pallor hidden by careful make-up and all traces of tears gone.

'Freddy was looking for you!' someone told her, and she nodded and managed a smile, then went at once to Freddy's office.

'Nice to have Sam back?' he teased, and she pretended to laugh. 'Well, you're going to be too busy today to see him,' Freddy added. 'Sorry, love, but I have to send you off to interview the duck man—the one who's doing a research project on the ducks in London parks. I'd send Sam to take the pictures, but he's needed on something more up his street. This South American dictator who's over here is going to visit the House of Commons today, and Sam has met him, so I'm sending him along to try to get some really unusual pictures.'

Lauren felt a sharp jab of fear. 'Isn't that the guy who keeps getting death threats?'

'That's the one! And probably deserves them!' Freddy offered her a yellow slip with typed instructions on it for her morning assignment, and she took it absently, frowning.

'What if someone tries to kill him when he's visiting the House of Commons?'

'It would make big headlines,' said Freddy with a grin, and she shivered, as though the office had suddenly grown very cold.

'And Sam could get killed!'

Freddy looked into her angry eyes, his expression wry. 'So could anyone who happened to be around! Come on, sweetheart, we can't wrap Sam in cotton wool, even to make you happy! Go and do your job, and let Sam do his! And stop worrying. It isn't going to happen. Sam's more likely to get killed crossing the road.' He paused, then added even more drily, 'Far more likely!'

She knew he was right, but her imagination was rampant all morning, while she talked to a slightly crazy scientist by a lake crowded with flocks of raucous ducks. She found it hard to listen while her mind kept conjuring up visions of Sam being shot down by mistake, being caught in crossfire, hit by a sniper's bullet. He had led a charmed life so far, he had always survived—but what if today was the day the spell wore off?

She was relieved, later, on her return to the office, to walk along a corridor and catch a brief glimpse of Sam with the picture editor leaning over a table covered with blown-up glossy photographs. Then she saw someone else in there and recognised Patty's delicate profile, heard her high voice. What was Patty doing in there with them?

A chill ran down her back. Surely Sam wasn't seeing Patty again? She walked on into the newsroom, eaten with jealous suspicion. She knew Patty still liked him—but it hadn't occurred to her that he would pick up where he had left off with Patty. Perhaps he had liked her far more than he had been ready to admit? Perhaps...

Stop it! Stop it! she said violently to herself, hating her own thoughts. What good was it doing to think about it?

It wasn't her business; neither Sam nor Patty would thank her for interfering, any more than they had last time. She had her job to do and she had better concentrate on that.

She was just finishing her last story of the day, at around six-thirty, when her phone rang, startling her.

'Lauren, it's me,' Rob's voice murmured, and her eyes opened in surprise.

'Oh, hello!' she said quite normally, then frowned, her voice turning brusque. 'What do you want?'

'I have to talk to you. Could you stop off for a drink on your way home tonight? At my flat?'

'No, certainly not,' Lauren said tersely. He had to be joking! Anyone would think they were just old friends, that there was no reason on earth why she shouldn't just 'drop in' for a drink in his flat any time she was passing! Was he crazy? Or just hopelessly selfish? Didn't he even remember he had jilted her? And hadn't even had the courage to do it to her face, had simply written her a letter and left her sitting in the wine-bar waiting for him while he went off with his new woman. She no longer cared, she had realised she had never loved Rob anyway, but she was still breathless at his total lack of any sensitivity or decent feeling.

He sighed, as if disappointed in her, but didn't waste time arguing. 'I could come to your flat——' he began, and she interrupted.

'No, you couldn't. And if you did I wouldn't let you through the door!'

Impatiently, Rob said, 'Well, how about the wine-bar?'

'And have everyone in the building talking about it tomorrow?' Lauren said bleakly. As if they wouldn't have enough to talk about once they knew Sam had started seeing Patty again! 'What do you want to talk about, anyway? Tell me now.'

'I can't—I have to see you. Please, Lauren ... just a drink, for five minutes. Look, we could make it look like an accidental meeting. You go in and wait and I'll show up casually. Please, Lauren!'

He sounded so urgent; she couldn't refuse point-blank, so she wearily agreed, and half an hour later she ran across the road to the wine-bar.

It was a wet and windy night, people were probably going straight home, so for once there was almost no-body in the bar, and she didn't recognise any of the handful of customers. She picked out a table in a par-ticularly dark corner, ordered a glass of white wine flavoured with *crème de cassis* and settled back to wait, her eyes lowered to her drink.

Rob arrived five minutes later and stood looking around, did a rather too obvious double-take as he pretended to notice her, then walked over.

'Well, hi!' he said, too loudly, to make sure he was heard all over the bar. 'What are you doing here? Mind if I join you?'

Lauren glanced into the mirror hanging on the wall. Nobody was watching them, nobody cared.

'Sit down, Rob,' she said grimly, and he sat oppo-site her, leaning back in his chair. The waiter brought him a drink and he played with the glass, pushing it around the table, frowning at it.

'Well, what was so important?' Lauren asked after a moment of that.

'I'm really worried about you,' Rob said, in a voice she knew he wanted to sound quietly sincere. Instead it sounded phoney, but his face looked sincere enough. 'I feel responsible,' he said. 'It isn't like you to be so reckless ... I blame myself, and I'd never be able to forgive myself if something disastrous happened to you.'

'What are you talking about?' she asked, baffled.

'Sam Hardy,' he said, and she felt her colour rise, along with her temper.

'I don't want to talk about him!' She moved to get up and leave, and Rob caught hold of her hand and wouldn't let go.

'Lauren! How can you date him, of all men? You told me yourself that he was a flirt and couldn't be trusted!'

'But he *is* fascinating!' she said, just to be provoking, but she had to sit down again because if she didn't that would attract a lot of attention. She was furious. How dared Rob, of all people, give her lectures on how to conduct her life?

'And what if he dumps you the way he does everyone clsc?' asked Rob, and she lifted her furious green eyes to stare pointedly, reminding him that he was in no position to talk about dumping people!

He had the grace to blush and look down, but then he tightened his grip on her hand, muttering thickly, 'Lauren, you aren't sleeping with him, are you?'

She felt her skin begin to burn. She didn't answer, but Rob burst out jealously, 'You *aren't*? How could you? You would never sleep with me!'

'For sheer damned nerve, you take the prize!' she muttered, trying to pull her hand free.

'If it was anyone else I'd say good luck,' Rob pleaded. 'But not him... He's a brilliant photographer, and a swine with women. I don't like the man, and I wouldn't trust him further than I could throw him. Sam Hardy can only make you miserable—you know that. I realise you're on the rebound, and that it's my fault...but please, don't waste yourself on Sam Hardy, he isn't the man for you, Lauren!'

His voice had risen, there was a funny little silence in the wine-bar, and Lauren looked up, realising that everyone was listening and staring. Then she realised something else, and turned pale as she saw Sam walking towards them through the tables. He looked dangerous, the set of his shoulders a threat, his face taut and frowning

Rob saw him a second after she did. He drew breath audibly, turning pale.

Sam reached them and loomed over the table, his narrowed grey eyes staring at their linked hands. Rob let go of her as if he had been scalded.

'Outside!' Sam said to both of them, biting out the word between his teeth.

Rob stayed in his seat, white and rigid. 'Don't you talk to me like that!' he muttered. 'You seem to forget who I am ... You work for my family...you can't give me orders...'

'I can break your neck,' Sam said. 'Either outside, or in here—it's entirely up to you.'

Lauren got up, skirting Sam's menacing figure without looking at him, and walked towards the door. If there was going to be a nasty scene, she would far rather it happened outside where there was a smaller audience.

Rob scuttled after her, with Sam behind him. It was pelting with rain in the street; Lauren sheltered under a shop canopy next door, her eyes on the wet pavements, wondering whether to make a run for it to the taxi rank nearby. She should never have agreed to meet Rob, of course. It had been stupid. But that didn't give Sam Hardy any right to throw his weight around and bully her. She didn't care what he did to Rob, though. Rob deserved it.

'Well?' Sam snapped. 'What was going on in there? Can't you make up your mind which woman you really want, Cornwell? Maybe I'd better make it up for you!'

Rob thought he was going to hit him, and Sam did look violent, his face as hard as steel, his eyes glittering. Rob shot backwards, his hands thrown up in defence, stammering.

'I...d-don't...' He was scared of Sam, and Lauren could not blame him. In this mood, Sam was frightening; he frightened her too.

Sam's mouth twisted. 'Oh, don't worry, I'm not going to hit you!' he said with contempt. 'Although I'm tempted to, and maybe somebody ought to give you a damn good beating. If your father had slapped you a few times when you were a kid, you might not be a selfish little bastard now. You've done Lauren enough harm. Stay away from her in future. You can't have both of them—you can't have your cake and eat it too. It's time you learnt that. You may be Charlie Cornwell's son and heir, but that doesn't mean you can have everything you take a fancy to. Go back to Janice. She's too good for you, but for some crazy reason she wants you, and it suits your father to have you marry her, so for once in your life you'd better keep your word and do what you've promised.'

Rob opened his mouth as if to protest, explain, argue and then met Sam's icy eyes and closed his mouth again, deciding instead to flee. He dashed out from under the striped canopy into the rainy night, and vanished in the direction of the car park beneath the Cornwell building, where his car was always garaged.

Lauren felt he had made the right decision. Sam did not look very amenable to discussion. She debated how far she would get if she tried to run too, and glanced along the glistening pavement to the taxi rank.

CHAPTER TEN

SAM turned grimly towards her, as if reading her thoughts. 'Don't try it!'

'And don't you bully me!' Lauren muttered resentfully, hunched in her thin white raincoat, the collar up to hide her face.

'I haven't even started on you yet!' Sam's hand closed on her arm before she could get away. He began to walk across the road, very fast, in long, angry strides, pulling her after him.

'Let go of me! I'm not going anywhere with you! I want to go home, let go...' she babbled. He took not a blind bit of notice, and she wailed, 'Who do you think you are? You're hurting! Stop dragging me like that! Anyway, what right do you think you have? You're not my keeper. Bursting into the wine-bar, shouting, making a scene in public... it isn't as if you cared whether I saw him or not.' He didn't even look round, let alone argue, and the pain inside her chest made her voice harsh. 'And you're a fine one to talk! You and your women, going through them like someone using Kleenex...' She was talking wildly, feverishly, shaking from head to foot with a lethal mixture of pain and rage, but Sam didn't stop or look round—

she didn't even know if he was listening, although he couldn't help hearing because she was almost shouting now.

'You didn't even ask why we were together... why I was there with him... just walked up and accused us... attacked...' She was breathless now, stumbling, her feet skidding on the wet pavement.

They reached Sam's car, and he unlocked it with one hand, still holding on to her, and she went on muttering furiously, tugging at her imprisoned hand.

'Only a few months ago we saw you in the wine-bar with Patty, remember!' Was it only a few months ago? It seemed like a lifetime; so much had happened to her since that night. There was a bitter irony in remembering how she had felt seeing Sam with Patty. She had reproached Patty for being such a fool, for betraying her husband with a man like Sam Hardy!

It had never occurred to her that the tables would ever be turned and she would one day be sitting in the bar with Rob listening to him reproach her for sleeping with Sam, or that Sam would walk in and attack them both.

'A-and Patty's married,' she stammered. 'What about you and her? You were very sarcastic when I said you shouldn't date a married woman... You called me a prig, old-fashioned, puritanical... you've changed your tune, haven't you? I was just having a drink with Rob, and he isn't even married... he's just engaged.'

Sam turned savage eyes on her, his mouth a straight, hard line. He pushed her into the passenger seat with hands that did not try to be gentle, and slammed the door on her.

She tried to get out at once, but he was too fast for her. He leaned in, locked her door automatically from the dashboard before she got it open, and a moment later he was in the driver's seat starting the ignition.

Lauren could only sink back into the seat, fuming. 'And you haven't stopped seeing Patty either,' she raged. 'I saw you with her today——'

'I never started seeing Patty! I told you about that! She was unhappy and I made the mistake of being sympathetic and listening to her troubles. How was I to know she'd get the wrong impression?'

Lauren gave him a furious, scornful look. 'Oh, come off it, Sam! You know how attractive you are! You've had too much experience not to know the effect you can have on women!'

He grinned wryly. 'Not always deliberately, though! And as far as Patty is concerned I was the one getting chased. I didn't do any of the chasing!'

She wanted to believe him, and that made her even angrier. 'I tell you what I think! You only drop your women after you've managed to get them into bed. That's the game you play, isn't it? A little numbers game. You chase them until you get them and then you walk off, happily adding the new one to your score. How many is it now? You make me sick, I hate you...' She drew breath, trembling helplessly. 'I hate you, do you hear me?'

'I hear you,' Sam said bleakly, his eyes watching the road ahead.

Lauren's eyes had blurred with unshed tears. 'I want to go home,' she said in a husky voice.

'That's where I'm taking you,' he said, and his voice was remote. There was a frozen waste between them. Lauren felt very cold and sick; she wanted to lie down somewhere and weep, but she couldn't, so she just sat there in a terrible silence, wishing she was dead. He wouldn't forgive her for the things she had just said to him. From now on, they were going to be enemies.

When the car stopped, she dived out and began to run, but the pavements were slippery with rain and her feet skidded under her. She couldn't save herself and fell headlong. The impact almost knocked her out; she lay there groggily for a minute, face down in the rain. It was the last straw. She simply did not have the energy to get up.

Sam grabbed her arms and pulled her up, looked at her face, made a growling sound, then slung her over his shoulder in a fireman's lift. He put her down when they got to her front door, and held out his hand. 'Key!' he demanded tersely, and she fumbled for it in her bag. Sam took it and unlocked the door, then propelled her like a child into her flat.

'You need a bath,' he said, stripping off her wet and muddy raincoat.

'When you've gone!' she mumbled. Over his shoulder, she saw herself in the hall mirror—she was a mess, her hair darkened by rain, clinging to her scalp, her face pale and muddy, a streak of blood on one temple. Why did Sam have to be there when she looked like that?

'Now!' Sam said, sweeping her off her feet again and striding down the corridor into her bathroom. He dumped her unceremoniously on to a chair, bent and turned on the bath taps.

'Get out!' Lauren was becoming alarmed.

Sam straightened, leaving the water running, and turned to her. 'Get your clothes off!'

She backed into a corner, flushed and agitated. 'Go away first!'

His mouth twisted sardonically. 'It won't be the first time I've seen you without your clothes, now, will it?'

'Go away!' she yelled, shaking, but he didn't go, he took another step, gesturing peremptorily.

'Will you stop arguing? Just look at yourself!' He turned off the taps, picked up a sponge from the side of the bath and the next minute began washing her face, as if she were a child.

She submitted to that, soothed and comforted, then let him gently towel her skin dry, which was a mistake, because he went on, before she could stop him, to begin undoing her shirt.

She tried to slap his hands away then, but he leaned on her with his entire body and made it impossible for her to move. 'Keep still!' he ordered, his face mere inches from hers, and she couldn't breathe suddenly.

Sam slowly undressed her in spite of her writhing protests; first her shirt and then her neat dark grey office skirt. There was a deliberate teasing in the way he stripped her, sliding the thin silk straps of her slip down over her naked shoulders, his fingertips cool on her skin, lingering on her, caressing.

'Don't! That's enough! Stop it!' she muttered as she
felt his fingers on the clip of her bra, but Sam undid it
and peeled it off, and then she was naked, and he was
looking down at her, breathing audibly, thickly. Her
skin was burning, her body tense, she had to close her
eyes because if he saw the look in them he would know
how fiercely she wanted him to touch her, even now,
and at all costs he must not know that.

His hand slid softly down her bare arm, brushed her
breast, sending an electric shock of intense response
through her. Lauren groaned helplessly, weak at the
knees as his head came down and his lips rested
warmly on her shoulder—and then Sam suddenly
lifted her off the floor and dropped her into the bath,
sending a tidal wave of water splashing over the rim of
the bath, on to the tiled floor.

Lauren gave a hoarse cry of shock, grabbing the
sides of the bath. When she had recovered she found
she was alone. Sam had gone. On a reflex action she
scrambled to the end of the bath and bolted the door,
and heard his dry laughter outside.

'Bolting the stable door after the horse has gone,
Lauren?'

She sank back into the warm water and closed her
eyes, waiting for the trembling in her body to stop before she began washing herself. She stayed in the bath
for some time, relaxing; afraid to get out because she
didn't know whether or not Sam was still in her flat.

At last she had to get out because the water had
chilled, and she was getting goose-pimples. She tow-
elled herself lightly and looked around for her clothes.

But they had got soaked when Sam threw her into the bath and sent water everywhere, so she couldn't possibly put them on again. Reluctantly, she had to put on the towelling robe hanging behind her door, then she padded out and made for her bedroom.

Sam was lying on her bed, full length, his arms behind his head, his long body casually at ease, watching her mockingly as she stopped dead in the doorway, his grey eyes roving from her damp hair to her damp, bare legs and feet.

'Why haven't you gone? I want you out of my flat!' Lauren flung at him, and he swung his long legs down and stood up, which somehow made her far more nervous because the faint smile had gone and his eyes were dangerous as they watched her.

'I don't give a damn what you want!' he told her through lips which barely parted to let the words out. 'I have a few things to say to you, and I'm going to say them. And you're going to listen!'

'Don't waste your breath! Whatever you've got to say, I don't want to hear it.'

'That's too bad! You're going to have to! You keep flinging accusations at me, but when I try to answer them you refuse to listen!'

'If you're talking about Patty, OK, I believe you. Now, just go away and leave me alone!' Lauren held the door open pointedly.

'Why do you keep on doing this to me?' he snarled, coming towards her. 'One minute I think I'm finally getting somewhere with you, and the next you're gone, and I never know why, or what I've done.'

'I wasn't the one who left the island the morning after Mel and Johnny's wedding without a word!'

'My note explained——'

'There wasn't any note!'

His brows met. 'I left one for you at the hotel desk!'

She stared, not knowing whether to believe him or not. 'I didn't get any note,' she repeated. 'I woke up and you'd gone! What was I supposed to think?' Bitterness grated in her voice, as she looked at him with hatred. 'All I knew was that you'd been trying to sleep with me for a long time, and now you had—and you couldn't even be bothered to wait for me to wake up, to say goodbye!'

Sam had flushed darkly. 'You were sleeping so deeply. I couldn't bear to wake you, and I couldn't wait, I had to hurry to get that plane back to London. There wasn't another one for twenty-four hours, and Freddy wanted me back as fast as possible because a couple of the photographers had called in sick and the photo desk was very short-handed.' He stared at her, frowning. 'Lauren, I did leave a note at the hotel reception desk! I don't know why you didn't get it!'

'Why didn't you leave it in my room? Or push it under my door?' she countered disbelievingly.

'It never occurred to me,' he admitted slowly. 'I'd woken up before dawn, and tiptoed out, so that I wouldn't wake you . . . and then I rang Freddy, and from then on I was in a tearing hurry to get back to London. I knew you planned to stay on for a few more days, and I didn't want to wake you unless I had to.'

She wanted to believe him, and that was the craziest folly of all. Roughly she said, 'Anyway, that doesn't explain why there wasn't a single word from you after I got back—you didn't write, you didn't ring. Silence. That was all, just silence! So don't tell me that I was the one who walked out on you, because it was the other way around.'

Sam hesitated, then grimaced, shrugging in a defensive way. 'I'm sorry, Lauren; it didn't even occur to me. When I'm working, I don't think about anything else. That's the sort of guy I am—I've been accused of having tunnel vision, and there's something in that. All I think about is my work when I'm doing it. That's one reason my relationships always seem to break up. Women resent having to compete with a camera for my attention.' He looked at her with hesitation, his eyes vulnerable, uncertain, and Lauren couldn't believe what she was seeing in his face. 'And even if I did remember to get in touch...you see, I hate writing letters, I never write them if I can help it—and I don't make phone calls either, except when I have business to do, something important to say, and then I keep it short and sweet.'

'Oh, that's wonderful!' she snapped angrily. 'You can walk out on me without a word and stay away for weeks on end without bothering to get in touch, and I mustn't complain! Well, as far as I'm concerned you can stay away for ever. I never want to see you again!'

He visibly stiffened, flinching, his eyes darkening, almost black, the pupils enlarged so that they seemed to take over the whole eye. 'Do you mean that?' he asked harshly.

Lauren opened her mouth to say yes, but the look in his face silenced her and she bit her lip, her glance falling. If he was indifferent to her, why did he look like that? Her mind was in turmoil; she desperately wanted him to care, but she was afraid of her own need.

Sam caught her chin in one hand and tipped her head back, staring down into her restlessly shifting green eyes. 'Why did you walk out on me that first time, Lauren? I never understood what went wrong. I'd begun to think I'd finally met a woman I wanted to stay with for the rest of my life, and then suddenly... pow! You were gone. Why?'

'I didn't want to be just a number in your list of conquests!' she said with bitterness. 'Ironic, really. I managed to put it off, but you got me in the end, didn't you?'

'I made love to you because I love you,' he said, and the rough depth of his voice sent a shudder through her. She looked up into his eyes and was very still, longing to believe him.

Sam went on huskily, 'I'd never been in love like that before. However much I liked a woman, it never went very deep with me. It was always something I could walk away from without looking back, and I'd stopped expecting ever to fall in love. I didn't even believe in it any more. I thought it was just a fairy-story for romantics. Then I met you, and I fell in love within days. It was like being knocked out. I was dazed by you, light-headed, I'd never been so happy in my life.'

Lauren was listening as intently as though her life depended upon it, and it did. If Sam was telling the truth, her whole life would be so different.

'I thought you felt the same,' Sam said, his skin very pale, and she wanted to tell him she had, she had loved him exactly like that, with a wild happiness and surprise that had made her feel she was walking on air, but she had been hurt too much the morning she woke up and found him gone—she wasn't going to risk trusting him again just yet. She bit her lip and listened, trembling with hope and passion.

'I was devastated when you walked out on me,' Sam said harshly. 'I thought there must be some misunderstanding. I rushed round here to see you, and you were...' He broke off, his face grim, then said flatly, 'Well, you know how you were! Icy, distant, a totally different woman... I knew the door had been slammed in my face. That was the worst day of my life. I didn't know why you'd changed, but I thought there must be someone else, or that you'd never cared the way I did in the first place. I had to accept that it was over, and it hurt. I had to get away from London. The only way I could forget you was to bury myself in work and never look back, which was what I did until I was hit by that bullet and put into hospital for months.'

Lauren shivered, sick at the realisation that he might not have survived.

Sam looked sombre too. 'I had plenty of time to think while I was lying in that hospital bed. Coming that close to death gave my whole life a new perspective. I kept thinking about you, realising that my life didn't mean much without you. I came back to work determined to see you again, and try to talk you into marrying me. I'd no sooner got back than I heard that you were dating Rob Cornwell, and then I saw you—and you looked at me as if we were total strangers. I had to face the fact that you didn't even like me, let alone love me.' His face tightened and his mouth twisted. 'Then you got engaged to Rob, and that was the second worst day of my life.' He stared down into her eyes, his voice deepening. '*Did* you love him, Lauren?'

She shook her head and said with dry honesty, 'Not really, although I tried to convince myself I did. Oh, not because he was rich, although it impressed me and made me feel pretty special, going out with Charlie Cornwell's son. I could never quite forget Rob was the son of our boss. But that wasn't all there was to it! I was attracted to Rob. He's fun and he's good-looking, and I was on the rebound from you. I wanted to find someone else to love because I was afraid I would never find anyone I cared about as much as I cared about you.'

She heard the intake of his breath, saw him pale and then flush, his grey eyes eating her face. 'Lauren! Are you saying...?'

He framed her face in his hands and for a moment she thought he was going to kiss her, then he burst out harshly, 'But if you did care...why did you leave me?'

'I heard about your reputation,' she said, and Sam's face tightened. Lauren looked contritely at him. 'I'm sorry, but I was feeling very uncertain of myself, and of you too. I couldn't quite believe you really cared for me, and when I met someone who knew you very well——'

'Who?' he demanded, scowling.

'I'm not going to tell you that, because I know her well enough to realise it wasn't maliciously intended.'

Sam looked cynical. 'If she tried to turn you against me——'

'I don't think she did. She just warned me that you never dated anyone for long, and I suppose I was ready to believe it. It fitted other things I'd heard. People do talk, you know, and you've said yourself that your relationships never lasted.'

'No, that's true,' he admitted bleakly. 'But it was different with you...'

She felt her heart turn over with a happiness that was almost frightening, but she said with a catch in her voice, 'How could I have known that? I only knew that you had this reputation. I couldn't bear the idea of being just another of your women; I wasn't waiting for you to get tired of me and drop me. So I walked out on you before you could do it to me.'

'I was in love with you!' Sam said with rough impatience, and Lauren put her arms around his neck and smiled up at him, radiance in her eyes.

'I didn't know that!'

Sam's arms went around her, too, convulsively. He held her close against him, his face almost touching hers, looking into her eyes.

'Lauren, I loved you then, and I love you even more now, because I know you better than I did. You're the woman I want to live with, the woman I want to bear my children.' He groaned aloud, darkly flushed. 'What more can I say to make you see I'm in deadly earnest? I want to marry you, Lauren...'

'Don't talk at all,' she muttered huskily, her finger-tips caressing his hair, his face, his throat. 'Sam...oh, Sam...'

The passion in her voice was like a match to dry grass; the fire flamed up between them instantly and there was no more talking for a long time.

When they lay on her bed together, close and relaxed, in each other's arms, Sam murmured, 'Isn't it time you told me that you loved me?'

'Didn't I?'

He laughed at the teasing look she gave him. 'You showed me, my darling—oh, yes, you showed me, but you never actually said it...'

She whispered into the warm skin of his chest, and he laughed, tilting back her head.

'Louder! I can't hear you!'

She lay looking into his eyes, her face growing serious. 'I love you, Sam,' she said again, this time aloud, with shaking intensity, and he kissed her, deeply, slowly, taking his time.

When he lifted his head her green eyes were drowsy and over-bright, and she lay curled up against him in silence, too happy to talk. It was Sam who broke their contented peace.

'This is going to be a bombshell in the office!'

'I don't think so,' Lauren told him. 'Everyone I meet these days seems convinced you and I are having an affair. Even Freddy... he was pleased because he wants us to work together; he says we're perfect partners...'

Sam laughed drily. 'How typical of Freddy. He believes we're sleeping partners, so he teams us up together at work! What a neat and tidy mind the man has! Which reminds me, talking of neat and tidy minds... Janice wants us to cover her wedding, did you know that?'

She nodded. 'She's suggested it to me. I don't mind, if you don't. I like Janice, she's got style, and you were right when you said she was too good for Rob. She is!'

'She's having a big wedding—all the trimmings, no expense spared.' Sam gave her a quick look. 'I suppose you want the same?'

'No, thanks. I'd rather have a quiet wedding... just family and friends... and a fabulous honeymoon somewhere exotic!'

'I can see you and I are going to agree on everything,' Sam said.

HARLEQUIN®

PRESENTS Plus

Meet Samantha Maxwell, a sensitive, naive and incredibly innocent woman, and Matthew Putnam, a man who's as rich as sin and about to ruin Samantha's life.

And then there's Andrea Markham, a concert pianist who's desperately attracted to her manager. But to what end—Luke Kane is a bachelor at heart!

These are just some of the passionate men and women you'll discover each month in Harlequin Presents Plus—two longer and dramatic new romances by some of the best-loved authors writing for Harlequin Presents. Share their exciting stories—their heartaches and triumphs—as each falls in love.

Don't miss
RICH AS SIN by Anne Mather,
Harlequin Presents Plus #1567
and
BACHELOR AT HEART by Roberta Leigh,
Harlequin Presents Plus #1568

Harlequin Presents Plus
The best has just gotten better!

Available in July wherever Harlequin books are sold.
PPLUS2

Relive the romance...
Harlequin and Silhouette
are proud to present

by Request

A program of collections of three complete novels by the most requested authors with the most requested themes. Be sure to look for one volume each month with three complete novels by top name authors.

In June: **NINE MONTHS** Penny Jordan
Stella Cameron
Janice Kaiser

Three women pregnant and alone. But a lot can happen in nine months!

In July: **DADDY'S HOME** Kristin James
Naomi Horton
Mary Lynn Baxter

Daddy's Home... and his presence is long overdue!

In August: **FORGOTTEN PAST** Barbara Kaye
Pamela Browning
Nancy Martin

Do you dare to create a future if you've forgotten the past?

Available at your favorite retail outlet.

REQ-G

Fifty red-blooded, white-hot, true-blue hunks from every
State in the Union!

Beginning in May, look for MEN MADE IN AMERICA!
Written by some of our most popular authors, these
stories feature fifty of the strongest, sexiest men, each
from a different state in the union!

Two titles available every other month at your favorite
retail outlet.

In July, look for:

CALL IT DESTINY by Jayne Ann Krentz (Arizona)
ANOTHER KIND OF LOVE by Mary Lynn Baxter
(Arkansas)

In September, look for:

DECEPTIONS by Annette Broadrick (California)
STORMWALKER by Dallas Schulze (Colorado)

You won't be able to resist MEN MADE IN AMERICA!